Whalesong

Whalesong

ROBERT SIEGEL

Crossway Books
Westchester, Illinois

Jacket and logo design: The Cioni Artworks/Ray Cioni
Jacket illustration: Scott Gustafson

First printing, 1981
Second printing, 1982

Printed in the United States of America

Library of Congress Catalog Card Number 81-66610
ISBN 0-89107-219-5

For the Whales,
great and small

Yonder is the sea, great and wide,
   which teems with things innumerable,
living things both small and great.

There go the ships
   and Leviathan which thou didst
      form to sport in it.

Psalm 104

Where great whales come sailing by,
Sail and sail, with unshut eye,
Round the world for ever and aye.

Matthew Arnold

Then one whale began to sing; and a second, and a
third. Soon the mewings, creaks, and whoops filled
the water. Some of the performers were close, and
some were far away. And, because of the underwater
canyon, the sounds echoed two or three times at
intervals of five or six seconds. It seemed almost that
one was in a cathedral, and that the faithful were
alternating the verses of a psalm.

Jacques Cousteau in *The Whale*

One

The first thing I remember is a dim green radiance, the deep lit by a single shaft of light, and the singing, always the singing. The dim green was wonderful, with my mother hovering over me like a cloud. Through a cluster of bubbles I would turn and swim in her milk, feeling the great warm pulse of her heart and the music growing louder and more various. The strains moved up my dorsal and wrapped themselves around my heart and told me things until my heart dissolved in light. Afterwards I would go to sleep on my mother's back, her flipper stirring a little current over me as her song lowered me into darkness.

The green deep was the most wonderful place then. The mothers hung over us like rain clouds while the sun fell about them in shafts leading to air and the world above. At first the other calves and I would just stare at each other across the bands of sunlight between the islands of mothers. Growing bolder, we would edge into the sun, touch the tips of our flippers, and flash back to the great safe shadows. Soon we were rolling and tumbling together through sunlit spaces in play that went on forever until the black of night closed over us.

Much of our time was spent on the surface. I can

still feel my mother's firm back lifting me toward it. The higher we rose the lighter the water became, with the sun warping and flashing above us. An instant later we'd break into that beautiful and perilous world at the top, with its blue sky that runs forever like the sea and clouds like albatrosses beating their way before the wind. And the light upon the waves—the sparkle and roll of them and the indescribable colors! There we'd remain until a low whistle warned us to slip under again, and we'd sink down, down into the luminous green, letting ourselves go, feeling the pull of the deep.

Sometimes we'd rest a while at the bottom, listening to our mothers croon or tell stories of the world above. These stories enchanted us and seemed unbelievable then: stories of winds that raised the waves high as mountains, of a light that split the sky in half, and of the great roar of Ohobo that always followed it. We heard stories of a world above the world of water, where whales could not go, and of monsters with red and green eyes that came from the other world, skimming over the surface, belching black smoke and devouring whales. We heard tales of our fathers off hunting for the shrimp called krill and shivered a little, looking forward to their return. Later my mother would nudge me to the surface and croon me to sleep, singing the rhyme that begins,

Around and over and under the sea,
Come, oh come, White Whale to me.

We slept, my mother on her side and I nestled between her long white flippers, rocking in the tropical night air. The stars against so black a sky made great gashes of light, blazing yellow and blue and red and green. Sometimes we lay near a mountain that rose beyond the water, part of that world where whales cannot go. And the smells—if only I could describe the smells! A perfume blew over us that wakened yearnings in me for I know not what. It was sweet and forbidden, because we could never go there. It blew from things I later learned to name fruits and flowers. Mother called the yearning *Hunger for the Land* and only laughed when I asked her why we couldn't go there. One day, she said, the Great Whale would explain.

All of us calves were by now skilled swimmers. I'd become good friends with Lewtë, a female a month older than I, but not much bigger. Lewtë had a rare albino streak along both sides and, when she did a barrel roll, was a flutter of white and black.

She and I used to leap over the backs of the mothers as they swam lazily along, scooping up plankton, heading toward a rendezvous with our fathers. We Humpbacks pride ourselves on breaching, or leaping entirely out of the water. Even adults—the cow and bull whales—will sometimes spend the whole day breaching, turning somersaults, and landing on their backs, sending the spray heavenward. But Lewtë and I made up a game that involved more than breaching. In our game we had to leap over every second back across the pod or herd of whales. If any adult was spouting a breath, we had to leap through the spout. All the calves playing this game at once made a sight pretty as a circus of dolphins. I was usually the leader.

First I'd swim to the edge of the pod and plunge into darkness under the moving white flippers of a cow; then I'd shoot upward through green sunlit water, breaching the surface at great speed. With a kick of my flukes and a dance of spray I'd fly over the barnacled back of another, coasting through her steamy spout, down with a crash into the green, through the cool shadow of a third, her flippers moving like ghostly wings. Up again and down I went until I was dizzy and lay floating to catch my breath.

I remember the day a school of flying fish joined us. They flashed all colors, thin and gleaming in the sun, and thought pretty well of themselves. They followed us under bellies and over and, no matter which way we turned, never bumped into us or each other. It was like flying inside a rainbow—red, green, yellow, and blue iridescence—while they laughed on all sides a high whistling laugh. "Catch us if you can!" they cried, "Catch us if you can!" But they were too fast for us. After a long afternoon they flew away, a rainbow mist against the setting sun, promising to come back the next day. Each of us settled down next to his mother, exhausted.

Lewtë and I could jump the farthest of all, and

sometimes at night we swam out from the pod, underwater, beneath a milky moon that stretched and shrank on the surface. A distance out we'd rise up and turn around. Full speed ahead we charged the pod, leaping over and under them, bellowing and slapping the water: up and over and down together, shoulder to shoulder, the spray from our flippers flashing like herring, until everyone was fully awake. How Hrōta, the old bull leader, would roar! Our mothers would whistle shrilly, cuffing us with a flipper and lecturing us on manners until they fell asleep.

It was hard to sleep on those moonlit nights, the surface everywhere glittering blue and the points of waves showing their diamond teeth. One night we made the mistake of jumping over Hrōta. His high back, all mottled with barnacles, was a challenge. A jump too low and we'd scrape our bellies raw. Well, the old blowhard was only pretending to sleep and, too late, I caught a glimpse of his wicked little eye and his crusty white flipper reaching toward me. I dodged that but wasn't prepared for the sea-quake that followed as his flukes fell like a mountain, lashing my tail. They shoved me down, down, knocking the air clean out of me. I lost sight of the surface and thought I was drowning. When finally I struggled back, I sped yelping for my mother, Hrōta's enormous bellow ringing in my ears.

Other nights the water crawled with phosphorous life that shimmered and flashed in the spray. Often the singing kept us awake. At this time we were traveling slowly into cooler waters, hoping to rendezvous with those fathers who had left to hunt for the great krill wilderness. My father and Lewtë's were among them. For weeks we followed a deep sea canyon toward the meeting place. All night the adults sang their songs, sending them echoing along the walls of the canyon far below, across vast reaches of sea to the end of the world.

Each whale had his own song, but none, I thought, equal to my mother's. Hers lasted a long while, beginning with a soft croon to which I'd sometimes fall asleep. Soon, however, it changed into trilling whistles like birds skipping about on a barnacled back or water that leaps and dances down a cliff, then to a long shivery moan that probed every sea cavern between us and the ice at the end of the world. This moan stretched and bent in every direction, sometimes higher, sometimes lower, and was the sweetest sound I'd ever listened to. Sometimes it reduced me to tears—I don't know why. The big oily drops fuzzed my vision and I would hide from Lewtë behind my mother's flipper. Last there followed a series of creaks and clicking noises, very sharp and fetching, which ended in one long whistle. At that my mother would pause and listen anxiously for my father's answer. All the pod would listen as one, but we didn't hear a thing.

Of course, I am describing only my mother's song.

All the other whales sang too. Listening to all of them at once it seemed I might float right above the waves on the sound. There were whoopings, moanings, bellowings, clickings, bubblings, creakings, gruntings, tootlings, keenings, groanings, hootings, hummings, and whistlings blent together in a symphony telling the whole story of whales and the sea.

Every whale would stick to his song and repeat it faultlessly. The longer he lived, the longer and more complex the song grew. Sometimes he would sing only a few notes from it, but later he would pick up exactly where he left off. As the years passed, the song grew with the singer until many lasted for hours. We calves made only short whistles and squeaks which grew longer with the months, but we waited impatiently for the day when each one would sing his unique song.

There were also sounds for ordinary talk. But Humpbacks love to sing, especially on a summer's night. Many times we sang the same song, the most common called the Song of the Season. This song would change from year to year. We had other songs that had lasted for years beyond count. I would lie awake on my mother's back near her blowhole, feeling the song well up within her, and watch the bubbles rise in a necklace to the surface.

I would press down next to her blowhole and close my eyes while her back resonated with song. I felt I was singing along with her as the croon rose from deep within and spooled out over the vast moonlit miles, moving with the lilt of a wave to reach, and echo in, the farthest sea-washed cavern. It was as if I were listening to some ancient song rise from the fiery center of the earth, as if the earth were singing to his bride the sea, of how her waves fell and clustered about his stony shoulders. And then, as the notes changed, the sea answered him, singing of the tang of salt air in the blowhole, of the smell that teased one to chase a flashing and vanishing form, but also of sleep soft and soothing that dissolved one in her cold arms forever.

One night after her performance I was almost asleep when a sudden vibration passed through my mother.

"Wake up, Hrūna," she said, nudging me. "Do you hear it?" I rolled over and noticed all the others were absolutely silent. I couldn't hear a thing, so I gulped three or four breaths and plunged as deep as I dared. At last I heard it. It was far, far off, the way I always imagined mermaid music in the tales. First there was just a shiver of sound, something that passed over and disappeared like the crest of a wave. But soon I heard a high distant whistle followed by a cluster of faint moans. Scared, I shot to the surface.

"What is it?" I asked. Lewtë was swimming round and round her mother, skipping over the waves.

"Your father!" Mother replied, her eyes gleaming. "Your father is coming."

I was at once excited and a little frightened, for I had never met my father, Hrunta. He left on the krill hunt before I was born. The males who remained behind to protect us acted distant and aloof—except for the time old Hrōta nearly drowned me. For her part Mother ignored them also. But I could see that she felt differently about Father. She was excited, moving her flippers in circles and blinking—now and then giving the water a thunderous slap with her tail. I felt a swelling around my heart and very proud—proud that my father was one of those chosen to hunt the krill, proud that he was coming home at last. The rest of that night Lewtë and I chased each other in circles while keeping up with the pod.

At dawn we sighted five silvery spouts on the horizon. All the pod whistled shrilly together. In a few minutes came an answering whistle. For a long while we raced silently on the surface while the distant forms drew closer. At last we saw five huge shapes rise from the water as one, white flippers flashing in the rising sun, and land with five enormous splashes. In a few seconds all the adults were greeting them. I hung back, on the edge of the circle, watching to see which one my mother went to. She swam up to the very biggest and they nuzzled, flipper to flipper, rolling for a moment on the water. Then they lay cheek by cheek, slapping the water and making happy little whistles and grunts that didn't mean anything.

Needless to say I was impressed by my father's size. I noticed that he, like Lewtë, had splotches of white along his sides above the flippers. But when I saw my mother act silly around him, I wasn't sure I would like

17

him. In fact, for a moment I almost disliked him. I felt she might forget me now that Hrunta was back. But when they swam over to me my feelings changed.

"So this is my son," Father said in a deep voice, eyeing me from flipper to fluke. He sounded proud and smiled an enormous smile, showing yards and yards of black baleen. He took me between his flippers and gave me a squeeze, wringing the breath right out of me, then leaped and threw me into the air, catching me neatly with his flukes and turning to face me. "We've got ourselves a prize, Hreelëa," he said. Mother smiled and snorted shyly.

Flattered and breathlessly excited, I could only squeak. I knew from that moment he and I would get along. I started off to tell Lewtë. We ran head on into each other, she jabbering about her father and I about mine, and we swam back and forth between them arguing over whose was the biggest and the best.

My father's flippers were longer than I was. He was gigantic and black, except where the albino splotches spread up from his belly and chest. His back was salted with barnacles and his beautiful bow-shaped flukes shone white underneath and scalloped along the back edge.

That night I went to sleep cradled between my mother and father. Now and then they'd both turn over, rolling me like a pebble between them. I'd laugh and scream with delight at the massage until I lay limp as a jellyfish.

18

Two

The next morning the five fathers approached old Hrōta for a long conference. At the end Hrōta swam silently away from the pod and did not rejoin us the whole day. That day we rested by a bed of plankton, feeding and playing.

The whole pod playing was an unforgettable sight. Besides being the finest singers among whales, Humpbacks are the best acrobats. We calves watched our mammoth elders plunge below the green deep, into the blue, down into darkness. In a minute or two they'd return, shooting toward the surface at a frightening speed. Up and up all five storeys of them would rise clear of the water and hang for a moment, glistening in the sun, before turning and landing on their backs. Sometimes they'd turn complete somersaults. The sound of the impact was like thunder. We calves would ride the waves they made, scrambling over each other to be near the next leap. Sometimes two or three adults leaped over and over each other, braiding a wake of waves that we youngsters rode for half a mile. Afterwards we practiced slapping the surface with our flippers and lobtailing, making sounds that would carry far over the horizon.

Tired, we'd stop and swim into the plankton—salty,

21

sweet, and crunchy against the palate. I'd open my mouth wide and, when it was full, force the water out between my baleen. Then I'd crush the shrimp and other things against the roof of my mouth and swallow them. With a flip of my flukes I'd lunge further into that mossy jungle and fill my mouth again. At first I was so hungry from exercise, I gulped it all down, but as my hunger went away I savored each mouthful. It was then I noticed the hundreds of different flavors lurking in that lovely salad. Each bite revealed new ones. As I grew older I came to appreciate the saying among Humpbacks: *Each mouthful is the same, yet each is different.*

That evening the sun set in smoking purple-and-red clouds fanning out over half the sky. We calves were deliciously exhausted and full, lying about on the surface in the center of the pod while our elders spoke to each other in low tones. The sky grew darker purple and the sun, a blood-red ball, sizzled at last into the sea.

At that moment a low and infinitely sad moan surprised us from beyond the circle. It was Hrōta's. None of us youngsters had heard such a note before and the oil started to our eyes. The adults apparently were expecting it, for they all answered back in chorus the same melancholy note. The vibrations went all through me until it felt as if my insides had opened up.

Caloon, Caloon, they sang, and a slow tide of grief rolled back from the circle to Hrōta on the lonely outside, half a mile away. From the high heroic words of the lament, we calves picked up the story that our fathers had kept from us their first night back and that whole spectacular, romping day. Caloon, Hrōta's only son, had gone forth with the hunters of the krill but had not returned. We learned that the stories about monsters belching fire and smoke and skating on the surface of the sea were not just stories—they were true. The monsters had eaten Caloon. Smoke and fire and a long serpent had burst from one's mouth and bitten Caloon; then the serpent had hauled him fighting and foaming and bleeding over the waves. A larger monster—larger than many whales—swam up, opened its mouth, and swallowed him even as he thrashed the sea bloody. The other five whales rushed to help him and another serpent almost bit one of them. Soon more monsters came to chase them. Discouraged, their hearts heavy as stones, they dove and fled into the black depths.

All of this was strange to us, and we lay shivering in the middle while the elders, in a circle, sang the chorus to Hrōta's lament. The lament told the story of Caloon's begetting, his birth (his mother, Hrētha, had died bearing him), and the days of his calfhood as his father's pride and joy. It told of his Lonely Cruise and what he discovered on it and of his return to the pod to lead the hunters of the krill. The hunters sang of Caloon's exploits, especially of his killing a great shark one night. Caloon had yet taken no wife and was the

23

last of Hrōta's family. Hrōta was old. He had outlived them all.

Sadly his song came over the waves:

> *Gone is he from the great sea, gone from the restless waves,*
> *Caloon the keen warrior, comfort of an aging heart.*
> *Now will he never return where narwhal spears the blue,*
> *Where dolphin and seal dart, and herring dance in shoals.*
> *Now may the mermen moan, salting the sea with tears.*
> *No more will shark and squid shy from his powerful flukes,*
> *No blithe cow and bonny bear his happy calf—*
> *Only a slackening sire to sing his vanished song!*

He was answered by the others:

> *Wide is the sea we cross—or narrow, as One decrees.*
> *Come, my brother, close, and comfort you by our side.*
> *Sore is the single heart with none to share its hurt.*

Then all together:

> *Take him, Bender of Tides, who take the ocean in tow,*
> *From whose mouth flow waters out of the fathomless Deep,*
> *Over that Ocean of Light, where no one living may go.*

These are but a sample of the verses they sang. The song went on all night until the surface ran slick with tears and the mourners lay exhausted. At dawn they huddled around Hrōta, heads pressing his sides, and slept away the day.

With the fathers home, the long journey to the great krill beds proceeded at a faster pace. The waters were cooler now, the air brisker. We calves frisked along at a giddy rate and often spent the whole day away from our mothers.

I remember the dim green morning my father woke me with a brush of his flipper.

"Shhh," he whispered, the breath visible above his blowhole, "Don't wake your mother!" Shivering in the cool air, I swam after him. A few whale-lengths from the pod he turned and faced me, his mouth solemn, but his eyes dancing.

"I want you to meet some friends of mine." At that he turned and sped down a long green corridor of ocean. I nearly bent myself double trying to keep up with him.

An hour later we sighted an island. Father *said* it was an island, but it looked to me like a bunch of rocks sticking out of the sea. The rocks were covered with black wriggling things. Father spouted a signal and we heard a chorus of barks. Then most of the black things disappeared into the sea.

In a moment we were surrounded by them, plunging under us, leaping over us, barking up a storm. They had sleek black coats and slapped the water with their flippers. Hrunta snorted joyfully as one swam right up to his eye.

"Siloa, it's you! Son, meet my old friend." I swam out from behind his flipper, and Siloa threw up his nose and barked. He had white whiskers and white hairs on his snout and was the leader of the sea lions, as they were called. He and Father fell into a conversation about weather, tides, and krill. I floated over to where some of the other sea lions were leaping in a great arc, three in the air at once.

When they saw me, they stopped and crowded round. Suddenly they began slapping me with their flippers—all over, belly to back, stem to stern. I'd never had such a tickling in my life and let out a hoot that sent them skipping over the sea toward the rock. "Come back!" I called, laughing, and just as suddenly they did.

This time I restrained myself, giving in to only an occasional snort while they continued to tickle. I found it was even more fun if I did a barrel roll, starting out slowly, then spinning faster and faster. The faster I rolled, the faster they slapped. Finally, weak from laughter, I plunged, careful not to lobtail, and surfaced a few yards away. Whiskered noses gleaming mischievously, some swam over and gently fastened mouths onto my flippers as others grabbed hold of my flukes.

"Roll!" they squeaked between their teeth. And roll I did! They'd never had such a ride. Round and round, hanging by their teeth, up they went into the sky and down through my blue shadow. The sun flashed on their sleek sides as they smacked the water. One by one they fell off, from exhaustion or opening their mouths to laugh, and lay, bellies up, giggling weakly on the waves.

Suddenly a warning trumpet blast from Hrunta shook the water around us. Two sea lion pups left behind on the rocks had decided to swim out and see what was going on. My father noticed them and was just telling Siloa when something flashed white from behind the island. I thought it was a white dolphin or Beluga whale. It was headed right for the two pups wriggling through the water.

With a roar and a slap my father swam off at top speed. In a second I saw why. What I'd mistaken for a dolphin opened a dark gash below its nose, and the gash was filled with sharp triangular teeth. It was a shark, a large white shark. I'd seen only the small gray kind before, which never bothered us. Squeaking helplessly I joined the sea lions swimming after my father.

We were too late. The shark had reached the pups and was circling for the kill, its white dorsal fin cutting the water like a giant tooth. The pups stopped, bewildered. A piercing shriek sounded and the shark hesitated. My father had whistled to frighten him off.

The shark didn't see my father until the last moment and then turned toward him, its ugly mouth stretched wide.

Hrunta plunged and snapped his flukes out of the water, lifting the shark with them. I saw the white form fly up into the brilliant sunshine until I thought it would never come down, arching high over the rocky island to splash on the far side. What happened to it after that nobody was sure. None of us ever saw it again.

The pups swam to their mother and father, who nuzzled them joyfully, barking, whooping, and scolding all at once; then they gave each a sharp slap and nuzzled them again. I was so proud of my father I could hardly bear it. I plunged into the blue deep, rose quietly under his belly, and nudged his flipper. His eye rolled down at me.

"Never trust a shark, Son, even though you're much bigger than it." He added that I needn't worry overmuch about them. Our only dangerous enemy was the Killer whale—in packs and wild with hunger—and, of course, man. Still, sharks had few brains and were unpredictable; they would attack anything weak or wounded. Blood in the water drove them crazy.

The adult sea lions gathered round and serenaded us with a chorus of barks, slapping their flippers together. I lay there trying not to look proud and listening politely (because they were really awful singers). Before these finished, twenty others surfaced, each carrying a fat fish in his mouth. Father politely opened his mouth wide. With a bark, each tossed a fish into it. (Sea lions can toss things about wonderfully. I have seen two play catch with a flounder). Then Siloa told me to open my mouth and I ate the last five. Were they good! They were groupers—my first taste of fish of any size, and I have never forgotten the joys of that single mouthful.

Siloa escorted us back to our pod. The sun was setting when we arrived. My mother swam out to meet us and nosed me anxiously from chin to flukes while Hrunta recounted the day's adventures. The way he played down the shark episode disappointed me. Looking more anxious by the moment, Hreelëa asked him if it were wise to take me that far from the pod. I didn't hear his answer, for I couldn't wait to find Lewtë. She stared round-eyed as I told her the story of the shark. I exaggerated its size a trifle, deciding the story wanted some dressing up after the way Father had minced it to Mother.

"And your father knocked it across an *island!*" Lewtë exclaimed as I finished. She whistled and shivered to the tips of her flukes. For the time being I had won the debate about our fathers.

While we traveled toward the feeding grounds that spring, Hrunta took me on other expeditions. He taught me to hunt for krill, to dive down into the black deep and stay there for a long time, to organize a pod for defense, to navigate by song through the long sea-canyons, and to recognize the many peoples of the sea. He introduced me to walruses, elephant seals, grampuses, narwhals, gulls, terns, cormorants, albatrosses, and a dozen kinds of dolphins (there must be scores of different kinds) and occasionally to one of the other families of great whales. I was growing all the

29

time and Hreelëa stopped nursing me, saying that fifty gallons of milk per day was her limit. I ate more and more on my own, gaining fifty or sixty pounds a day— a ton a month.

Three

Several months later we entered cold waters, not far from where the world ends in mountains of ice. Even now I can taste my excitement as we entered those seas. Our spouts were visible in that air. When Hrunta surfaced from the black deep, his breath rose yards into the sky, hovering there like a white fountain. Mists stole across the water. Sometimes at night we'd glimpse a great albatross, whiter than the mist, winging across the moon, uttering his lonely cry. Occasionally an iceberg floated past. I still remember the first dark shape of one looming through the mist. I was frightened. But before I could flee, the mist parted and there floated an emerald mountain. I cried out and the cry went on for a little. I think that was the first time ever I sang.

And the krill! Long before we came to the ice we reached the great beds of krill the others had found for us. Krill are the best-tasting of all shrimp and live by the billions in beds of plankton. The reddish-brown krill stretched for miles and reached down into the deep half a mile. All one had to do was open his mouth and swim into it, munching. There were days I became lost in the krill, swimming forever to find my way out, my stomach so full I thought I couldn't move another stroke. We Humpbacks shared these beds with Fin whales and Blue whales and had to be careful not to run into them in the blind mass of shrimp. The Blues and Fins are larger than we, but do not sing nearly as well. Throughout that enormous larder you could hear the whistles, grunts, and snorts of whales heaving through an ocean of food.

Shortly after we reached the krill I passed the half-year mark, and Father hinted it was time for me to visit Hralekana, the most ancient of Humpbacks and the hugest in all the deeps. It was rumored he was larger than even the largest Blue whale. Hreelëa protested that I was still too young, but Father insisted.

"Hrūna is big for his age," he said, "and will one day be leader of a pod."

One morning not long after, we left the pod and swam for three days, resting only at night in the plentiful krill. I felt much curiosity about the Great Whale, as he was called, but also dread. Hrunta didn't say much or sing during this trip, but now and then I'd catch him gazing at me thoughtfully.

One morning I heard a strange song, a single low note sung over and over.

"That's Hralekana," Father said. "We're near. Take many deep breaths. We'll be under longer than ever before."

I breathed deeply as we swam on a short way. My father drew in a deep breath and plunged, his flukes beckoning me to follow.

Down into the green deep we went, Hrunta already small below me; down deeper into the blue; then down, down into the black deep where he vanished and we kept in touch only by sound. I felt the water close in about me, heavy and cold. I had never been down so far. Something long and slimy brushed past me and I nearly panicked. Lights appeared, strange lights, as glowing fish passed by in schools—strings of lights waving on tentacles, luminous three-sided creatures, and all manner of floating and winking shapes. These shrank above us like stars in the night sky. Still we dropped. The pressure rang against my ears and my lungs felt cold and leaden when Father entered a hole in the ocean floor, an underwater cavern. By the echo from its walls I knew it was huge. And I was afraid.

All that time the singing of the one note grew louder. The cave tunneled into darkness. At long last we saw a dim light at the far end. We emerged into an enormous underwater chamber whose walls, ceiling, and floor glowed—whether with plant or rock I to this day do not know. Ridges of pointed stones hung down in that eerie light like rows of teeth or baleen. But to tell the truth, I didn't notice them long, for there *he* lay.

Like some mountainous part of the rock itself, Hralekana stretched the length of the cave, his belly on the floor and his tail toward us. His back was warted and bumped, crusted with centuries of barnacles. Only here and there, where he'd rubbed them off, did a whitish patch of skin show through. His white flippers were the only part of him free of barnacles. Each much longer than I, they stirred in time to his song. He seemed not to notice us, though his eyes were open while the *oon oon oon* continued.

Even my father appeared dwarfed as he cleared his blowhole and addressed the Great Whale. The song ceased, and in a voice surprisingly soft, yet distant and austere, Hralekana welcomed us and asked us to draw closer. He shifted himself about and listened while my father explained the reason for our coming—which I myself did not know. Hralekana lay there a long time, regarding us from behind his wrinkled chin and enormous, knobbly jaw. At last he blinked and pointed a flipper at me.

"It is not often that one so young comes to hear the Story," he said, "though all come to me in their youth. So it has been for years beyond count." He paused. And I wondered if what they said of him was true, that he had lived the lifetimes of many whales. He was larger than any Humpback had a right to be and may well have grown for centuries. I shivered and drew closer to Hrunta.

The Great Whale continued: "So has the Story been passed down by those before me, and so will it be passed down by those after me until the seas run dry." He settled himself lower and smiled. I wasn't prepared for his smile. A wall of ivory baleen, stained and broken, rose before me and stretched into shadow on

36

either side. I felt like a krill about to be swallowed.

Just as quickly, he frowned. "Do not forget what I am about to tell you. It is a sacred charge."

And I knew that I never would, nor could.

He was silent again; his eyes took on a distant look. Then in a deep voice he told, or chanted rather, what I have never forgotten.

"In the beginning all was ocean, except for the sky and the great lights that swim across it. All creatures lived in the ocean, but they were far different from you and me and none can tell what they were like.

"The seas shrank, and here and there the bones of the world dried, and some creatures began to hanker after the dry places and to creep upon the land. At first they stayed only a little while, returning to their mother the sea, but after a time some stayed a long while, forgetting the sea. These became strong and grew jointed flippers to carry them about. Meanwhile, seaweed crept upon the land and plants tough as coral towered to great heights.

"At first the creatures were happy, but then they grew to be too many, for food on the land was scarce. And creatures who were kin learned to fight over the food and to kill and devour one another. They grew large and could do many wonderful things on their jointed flippers, but there was a sadness among them. A few felt a yearning for something they had lost, something they had forgotten, though they knew not what.

37

"One day a wandering tribe discovered the ocean. They were struck with wonder, because they knew nothing about the sea, their fathers having forgotten her. For many days they stayed by the shore, smelling the salt breeze and feeling strangely comforted, yet restless. At last, climbing the rocks, one fell into the sea and discovered he could swim, and even go under the water. The others cried out in terror, for they thought he had surely drowned. But when he came up again, they marvelled, and soon all were in the water. They settled by the ocean and, as generations passed, became great swimmers, going out ever farther and for longer times.

"The young with the strongest limbs were the best swimmers. Gradually they changed shape to move easily through the currents and waves, and their limbs turned into flippers and flukes. They learned to feed in the sea and to stay underwater for a long time. After many ages they lost the desire to crawl back on land. They became the many families of whales and dolphins, living mostly at peace with each other and eating the plentiful food of their mother the sea.

"Yes," he shifted, releasing a swarm of bubbles, "they answered the call of the sea and they—more than those who never left her—know what that call is.

"Thus for thousands of years they lived in peace, fearing no one, since whales are so large that few dare attack them. Whales had not yet encountered man, except when they now and then swallowed one by accident, mistaking him for a fish. Even then they were gentle with him and spat him out safely on shore. So it was until the Change."

Here he paused and frowned as only a Humpback can, the wrinkles in his chin drawing in to fierce creases.

"About the time I was born, all changed. Man had learned to build great wooden monsters to sail upon the sea. Pushed by the winds, these monsters moved swiftly. Still the whales were not afraid, and many swam close to the ships and boats, as the monsters were called, to see them.

"But man began to slay the whales with long shafts of wood fitted with metal teeth. They would stick these harpoons into a whale and fasten him to a boat with a serpentlike thing called rope. In vain would the whale swim and dive until he tired; then the boat would pull alongside and the men pierce his heart with long knives. As he died, rolling and thrashing in agony, singing his death song, the water turned red. Last, the men cut the whale in pieces and took him aboard the ship."

He stopped and, moved by some dark memory, moaned for a long minute. "This I saw when I was young. So died my mother and my father. Sometimes—wickedness upon wickedness—men would spear a calf and use its wounded cry to draw the maddened parents near to harpoon them." He choked and paused a long time while his face grew darker in that dark place.

My father, who had heard this story before, said gently, "Tell us, O Great One, what you did next."

A red fire gleamed in the depths of the Old One's eye. "I rose in my wrath—even then I was larger than most whales. I rose and seized one boat in my jaws and overturned it. Two others I splintered with my tail. In my anger I dove and rose under the large ship. I rammed its bottom at full speed and heard the timbers crack. The blow knocked me out. Later I came to on the surface with a terrible pain in my head. Except for a few spars floating about, the ship was gone.

"But my pod was gone too, and the loss of my family left me crazed with anger. Now it was I who hunted the whalers, and not they who hunted me. Often I would rise unseen to overturn their boats. Several times I was harpooned and pulled the boats under. I was joined in my hunt by our cousins the Blue and the Sperm whales. A large Blue swam with me many years and for a while we were aided by a Sperm whale. He was white like me and also larger than others of his family. We three were the scourge of the whalers. But the Sperm whale was careless, letting himself be seen, and gained a reputation that I fear was his undoing. To this day I do not know what happened to him; there were rumors he was hunted down by a crazed man. The Blue lived to a ripe age and passed on into the

Ocean of Light. Once again I was alone. But our people throve, despite the whalers, who were few and did not come very often.

"Alas, in later years it was not so. Man learned to make larger monsters—much larger—of metal and fire. These ships are many times my size and none can even dent them. They belch fire and smoke and spit a harpoon many yards into a whale's vitals, where it explodes and kills him, sometimes before he can sing his last song. The monster ships swim faster than whales. Like us they send out sounds and listen to the echoes and so are able to track us under water.

"They hunt us without pity and without sense. Our people are vastly diminished—a fraction of the number of old. Now the hunters often go hungry because we are so few in number. Now they must hunt porpoises and dolphins to fill their metal stomachs. As we whales diminish, so does the number of hunters. Soon there will be no whales and soon no hunters."

Here he paused even longer. I thought he had finished. His story and the cold water left a heavy leaden chill on me. My lungs began to ache from being under so long, and I felt woozy from lack of oxygen.

Yet he spoke again, this time lower than before, in a strange, dreamlike tone.

"After the Change I left the surface to come down here and be alone, to dwell upon the mystery of man and whale in my thoughts, to sing, and by singing discover the truth.

"Of late, ever and anon in the long night of this place I glimpse a light—perhaps a gleam from the Ocean of Light—and I know the end is near. Either the end of the slaughter or the end of whales and sea and earth as we know them. Lights from that Ocean tell me things I could never know, things that happen on land and in the sky above. Things . . ." he faded into silence and cleared his blowhole, "things I am forbidden to tell the whole of.

"And so my message to you, Hrūnakyana"—and here he pronounced my name, my full name, which I had never heard before—"is to live bravely, in hope, and to guard well cow and calf."

His eyes faded far away, and the faint tremor of a smile twitched across his huge face. "Yes, guard cow and calf well, and when in danger seek the singing of the ice at the end of the world."

Finished, he slowly turned his back on us. My father nudged me and we swam up the dark tunnel; its opening shone faintly gray. I needed no urging. My lungs were bursting and I felt faint. Just as we left the tunnel we heard the low *oon oon* of the Great One's song begin, striking the fundamental note of earth and sea.

Four

Desperate for air, I struggled toward the surface, relieved when at last it glowed dimly above me—only to find the glow came from the strange electric fish we'd passed on the way down. My heart failed me—the surface was still thousands of feet above. I breathed out a few bubbles.

"Courage, my son!" It was Hrunta. His huge back rose under me, rushing me upward. The water grew warmer, then dim blue. I was in the blue deep. With my last strength I climbed into the green deep, the golden surface winking just out of reach. I bent my flukes one last time, giving them my all. Then it was sky and the sweetest breath ever taken and Father spouting loudly beside me. The two of us lay speechless for an hour listening to the music of three gulls who circled and picked sea-lice from our backs.

Lazily we swam back to the pod, feeding on krill and pondering all that Hralekana had said. I thought of my complete name and the mystery of its meaning, and I knew that I was not the same calf who dove with my father earlier that day. Now I was Hrūnakyana—a name I would not hear spoken again but on the most solemn occasions. Mostly I thought of our people and their vanishing numbers. My heart felt sad and yet

45

buoyed up by hope, by the light in the Old Whale's eyes. I was to guard well cow and calf and in danger seek the singing of the ice at the world's end.

The others were glad when we returned. During our absence they'd seen a disturbing sight. They'd been wakened in the night by the cries of a Fin whale mingled with the sound of a ship's propeller. Several had followed at a distance, moving in close at dawn. They found a ship of strange shape towing the Fin alongside. Swimming closer, they saw he was tied with many ropes, but otherwise unhurt. They asked what had happened, but the frightened Fin could only cry *help* over and over. They left when men pried open his mouth with a hook and poured in a pail of dead fish. None of the pod knew what any of this meant.

The next three months proved uneventful, except that I played less with Lewtë, spending much time exploring the sea about us and going on short hunting trips alone. The waters had turned colder and storms came more frequently now. The elders knew summer was over and it was time to move back to the warm seas of our birth.

Some of the cows had grown very big indeed and ate enormous amounts of krill as they prepared to cruise toward the island shallows where they would calve. The whale couples who weren't expecting passed more and more time together at a distance from the pod. Sometimes I glimpsed a pair plunging into the black deep. A few moments later they would reappear, shooting toward the surface at an incredible speed, and together leap high out of the water, slapping each other with their long flippers. It was all very beautiful and mysterious and the rest of the pod pretended not to notice. Humpbacks mate for life, and each adult had a partner, except for old Hrōta. I felt sorry for him as he swam alone, leading the pod into warmer waters.

Then we were back in those warm and lazy seas, and the cows were searching out the best of the island shallows for their nests. The bulls were already discussing next year's migration, pleased we had escaped notice by the whaling fleets last season. I was growing more restless by the day. I had reached more than half my full size, and the games of calves no longer appealed to me. I took to going out on longer and longer trips, singing to myself and listening to the echo of my song rebound from the bottom of the sea.

One day Hrunta confronted me. Eying me keenly from flipper to fluke, he smiled. "You are going to be larger than I," he said. "Already your flippers are half as long as mine." I was pleased but tried not to show it. Calves were always wriggling and leaping when they were praised. And I was no longer a calf. But his smile faded as Hrunta continued, looking at me searchingly. "It is time for you to go on the Lonely Cruise."

He said no more and swam abruptly away. I knew what he meant, and was proud, but felt a hollow cave open in my stomach. The Lonely Cruise was a trip every whale took at the beginning of adulthood. Sometimes he or she wouldn't return for one or two years. Sometimes he wouldn't return at all, joining another pod in his travels. That night I slept between my mother and father. Hreelëa sang her song through several times in a sad and lovely way. One part of me wished to cry out that I didn't want to go on the Cruise, while another part eagerly awaited the dawn.

In the gray early light I said goodbye to Lewtë, who was quiet and turned quickly away after we touched flippers for the last time. Then I nuzzled my mother and father and took off, not looking back. A mile out I did three leaps in a row and turned to watch as the pair of them did three, the spray flashing silver in the early sun. At last I turned and swam along the radiant green corridors of the sea.

The first three days I was alone, except for here and there a bird crossing the far reaches of sky. And though the hollow feeling didn't entirely vanish, I felt good there with the sun, the sea, and the blue sky edged with rain clouds hanging over unseen islands. I had no idea where to go, so I followed the sun. The world was all before me and I didn't care which part I saw first.

I knew that sometime during the Cruise I had to take the Plunge. But I wasn't ready for it yet. I'd been taught the Plunge was the most special and hidden part of a Humpback's life. It came at the beginning of adulthood and revealed to the young whale the direction of his life, the particular note of being the Spouter of Oceans sang at his conception. I knew that some-time during the Cruise I would take that Plunge, but I wasn't ready yet.

During those first three days, however, I meditated on the story of the ocean's beginning as I had heard it many times from both Hreelëa and Hrunta.

In the beginning the Spouter of Oceans swam alone in the ocean of his being. So great was his bliss that he said to himself, "I will share my joy with others, whom I will make like myself." At that he took a great breath and spouted ocean, earth, and sky—the moon, stars, and sun that swim in the sky—and every living thing.

And to this day the whole world hangs there while he spouts, for that moment and this moment are but one moment to him. All that we are and know is but the vapor of his breath and will be so until he draws it in and we join the ocean of his being, creatures formed to be like him and to swim forever in the Ocean of Light.

The green emptiness of the sea made it easier to chew over that story and to see things in it I hadn't seen before. I was almost sorry when, on the fourth day, I noticed a commotion on the horizon. At first I thought it must be rocks where waves broke and frothed, so white was the surface. Then I saw small leaping shapes and wondered if they were my friends the sea lions, far from the cold waters of their home. The fracas moved rapidly toward me and I swam to meet it. As it drew near, I heard the most outrageous din: whistles, grunts, sputters, titters, and snorts assaulted me from every side.

A blue bulbous head popped out of the water a few yards to my right.

"Hello—Goodbye," it said and ducked, splashing me. I heard a high whistling laugh as it sped away.

"A Bottlenose dolphin!" I exclaimed, recognizing the snout: "the clown of the ocean." In a second they were all around me, plunging, leaping, nudging, and splashing.

"Stop it!" I gruffed. They drew back, still laughing and tittering as if they'd done something clever. Then they were on me again till I thrashed my tail about. The dolphins swam too nimbly to be struck and enjoyed themselves thoroughly in the waves I made, returning to tickle me until we all were exhausted. To tell the truth, after three days alone I rather enjoyed the frolic, and when they began pitching flounder at each other I decided to stay for the feast.

After we had eaten (I was hardly full, but didn't mention it.) they settled down a bit and we talked. Dolphins speak very rapidly and are sometimes hard to understand. Great gossips, they carry the news of the sea. Since there are at least a score of different kinds, and all the kinds keep in touch, a school this size knew just about everything that was going on. The leader, Delphi, was bright sea-blue and more sober than the rest. He told me news he thought I'd be interested in, but the others kept interrupting him with their tidbits or laughter. Indeed, all talked at once. It was impossible to get a story straight the first time. Since every story was repeated at least twice in the course of the afternoon, the interruptions posed no problem. I learned all sorts of things. I learned that, as of yesterday, my parents and pod were in good health, and that two of the cows—Kalua and Hweena—had calved. When I asked about the Fin whale they all jabbered at once. He was being towed toward a coast to the east— not to be killed, but to be put in a large lagoon closed off by a giant net.

"He'll be with two of my cousins," a white dolphin explained. At this remark the others grew excited, leaping, standing on their tails, and jabbering about captured dolphins. It seems that men often trapped one or more and put them in a lagoon many leagues from there. The white dolphin had spoken through the net with his cousins, who were anxious to escape, but nevertheless said they were well treated. They were learning much about man.

For one thing, men gathered about in big schools whenever the dolphins played among themselves or leaped in the air. Some of the men would hold out a fish for a dolphin when he leaped or hold a hoop for him to leap through. All of them slapped their flippers together whenever a dolphin performed. Men could do many other clever things with their flippers. Their

51

flukes were divided in two and with these they crept about on land. In the water, however, they were more helpless than calves.

Men made short harsh noises to each other which some thought might be a rudimentary language. When the white dolphin repeated her cousin's imitation of it, all the dolphins whooped and laughed and turned circles. It was a while before Delphi restored order.

"Nevertheless," the white dolphin continued, in an injured tone, "they have even heard men sing." I perked up at the mention of singing. Apparently one day a female came to the lagoon and sang into the water through a shell tied to a rope. Her voice was low and scratchy, and the notes very short, but all the other men—males, females and calves—slapped their flippers when she was done. Her song was not what you'd call beautiful, the dolphins said, but to encourage her to sing more, they leaped, slapped their tails, and sang back, imitating the sounds. Now she came and sang to them every few days and the two dolphins could repeat by heart the notes of her song.

Finally an old dolphin, crisscrossed with scars, broke in. "That's all very well, but it is a mystery how a creature can be so intelligent and still cruel as a shark. We've all seen how he kills porpoises and dolphins wantonly in his big metal monsters, and all know how—if my large friend here will pardon me—he tears whales into little pieces.

"Why, some of us remember when man, like a crazed shark, spent years killing off his fellows with noise and fire like a volcano's. The ocean was full of terrible sounds, burning monsters, and dead bodies. I lay near one island and watched ships toss fire at it for a whole day until all the trees on the island were burnt. There was blood in the water. I pushed one wounded man to shore. Not many years after, men made a great ball of fire—brighter than the sun—that swallowed a whole island and killed every living thing in the sea for many leagues around."

This speech shocked everyone. The young dolphins sidled up to their mothers. For the only moment that afternoon, all were silent.

At last Delphi spoke. "It's true that man is very clever with his flippers, but I am afraid that he uses his intelligence for bad things. The greater a creature's intelligence, the worse the things he can do with it."

With that final word on the matter, all started talking again, and I learned what the weather was like a thousand miles in every direction, the condition of winter mollusk beds, and the latest migratory routes of terns. There was a tropical storm brewing to the southwest, they said and, oh yes, I should look out for a fleet of whalers moving into warm waters. Had I tasted the small squid that grew about the coral reefs?

As the sun returned to his sea-home, I said goodbye, politely refusing their invitation to spend a few days with them. Their constant chatter was making me irritable. I plunged gratefully into the darkening waters of night.

A few hours of solitary underwater swimming refreshed me, and I surfaced to sleep under a crescent moon. Dark clouds blew before it, making me restless for something distant and unknown. The wind brought sweet smells from an island hidden over the horizon, and I recalled breathing those smells as a calf lying next to my mother. For a moment I felt homesick—for just a moment—because the smells sharpened that yearning for something indefinable. I was pleased to be alone and grown up, alone and out hunting that something. I was glad to rest on the dark waters by myself, snuffing perfumed air. I looked out over the low waves in the moonlight, and each rose in a glittering smile.

Five

The next day passed uneventfully except for two flying fish who swam beside me a while. The sun was high and hot and I snorted and dove and breached as I swam. That night the moon again wooed me and the clouds passed like vague shapes of the future. I felt utterly content and fell into a deep sleep. Too deep, it turned out.

A loud noise woke me as something slashed my right side. I fluked, dove to the bottom, and twisted in a wide circle, looking up. A snakelike thing dangled fathoms down into the blue deep. Above it loomed a black shadow—the bottom of a monster-ship, I guessed. From the cable's end hung a large toothlike thing with cruel hooks. I hid in a kelp bed and watched as it was drawn up. Only then did I notice a burning along my right side, where the edge of the harpoon had grazed me. It was just a scratch, but I shuddered at how close I'd come to death. Worse than the fear was my shame that I'd let an enemy come so close to me in sleep. Chagrined, I sank into the black deep.

In a few minutes I surfaced for air and saw the ship. Black, it rose high out of the water, and stared with eyes of various colors. The waves parted before its sharp nose as it churned toward me. On the horizon I counted six more ships, one of them as big as four of the others—as big as an island—twinkling like a night sky in the early gray. I dove again and lay still at the bottom, conserving breath. The ship waited above me for a long while and then, just before my lungs gave out, mysteriously chugged off.

I swam on that day in heavy spirits, feeling ashamed and exposed, missing the pod terribly. I wondered if Hreelëa worried about me at all. I thought of Lewtë and felt bad for acting aloof toward her those last months. That evening I surfaced to find the ocean looking stranger than ever before. Greenish clouds hovered in the west. The air lay still, and the waves rolled heavy and oily. Around a nearby reef, fish squeaked at each other nervously and huddled at the bottom. Three palm trees on the strip of island near that reef stood perfectly motionless, silhouetted black against the green.

From way behind me, traveling through the water, came a dull boom. It sounded like one of the cannon the harpooners used, though their fleet was miles away, over the horizon. The noise added to my uneasiness.

The clouds in the west seethed. A moment later I saw an even stranger sight. A cloud dipped down and touched the ocean. I watched the cloud's thin tentacle snake toward the island and me while its top leaned across the sky like the head of an octopus. It was huge.

I was too amazed to be scared. Soon I could hear the noise of rushing wind, though the trees stayed motionless. As the cloud loomed closer, the noise grew louder. The ocean rose up at its foot and—this I could hardly believe—the cloud sucked the waves right up into itself. A tentacle of water hundreds of feet high writhed across the water directly toward the reef and me.

For a minute I couldn't move. At last, with an effort of will, I turned and plunged in the shallow water. Skimming the reef, I sped over a ledge and was just headed down into the deep when I felt myself sucked upward. Above me the surface foamed white. I panicked, kicking toward the bottom, struggling against the current as the waterspout passed over. Then suddenly I was free. Lightning flashed through the choppy surface as I settled to the bottom safe and snug, remembering the story my mother told of Ohobo, the great enemy of whales, who roared over the ocean with his jagged harpoon, hurling it here and there and raising great waves, but never finding the whales, who lay quiet at the bottom. Each time his harpoon flashed it made a loud noise, resounding through the deep. Listening to that noise comforted me and I fell asleep realizing that Ohobo's was not the harpoon I had to fear.

In the middle of the night an especially loud peal of thunder woke me and I risked surfacing to view the typhoon. It was awesome. When I first came up all I could see was black sky as the wind howled and blew spray in every direction. Ohobo's harpoon forked down the western sky and I saw, gathered around me like mountains, the heaving waves. One lightning flash followed another as I watched the black waves run and dance in a tormented ring. As they swept under me I rose up—hundreds of feet it seemed—to their very crests. There I glimpsed the flashing horizon, where waves shone sickly green under frothing spindrift. For a moment it was clear as day. Then the light went out and I coasted back down the wave. Once a large object bumped me and swished by, taking my breath away. I guessed it was a tree and knew I should go back under. As I rose to the top of one last wave, I saw something even more curious: a red light rose over the far horizon and hung a moment before going out. With that strange light glowing in my mind I dove to the peaceful bottom and went back to sleep.

In the morning it was raining, but the sea was calm. I swam over to look at the island. The three palms had disappeared—snapped off by the storm. A family of gulls flew about me, shrieking miserably.

I felt a strange impulse to swim back the way I'd come—perhaps I was curious about the red light. In a few hours something white gleamed on the horizon. It looked oddly familiar. Drawing closer, I recognized the giant whaling ship I'd seen yesterday. Just the top was above the water.

I approached cautiously underwater until I saw what

had happened. The typhoon had driven it upon a reef and the bottom was broken open. Rope, pieces of wood, and all kinds of things floated about it. The top part was unhurt, though rocking dangerously in the swell. It swarmed with men. Carefully I rose to get a look at them. I was, I confess, disappointed. Even though I knew they were small, I hadn't expected to find men so puny—all flippers and legs, like squids or octopuses. They saw me, too, because they started making noises and waving their flippers about. At that I fluked and swam a mile away. As I surfaced, I bumped into a piece of wood. I heard a tiny croak and examined it. Floating on the wood were two men creatures. One was pointing and squeaking and the other trying his best to hide. I believe they thought I was going to eat them.

I reflected on what they had tried to do to me the day before. My shoulder still hurt. But they were small and obviously helpless in the ocean. So I closed my lips gently over the end of the raft and started to push it through the water. One man flopped off and began to swim away. He was certain to drown, so I turned and followed. The other man made a sound at him, and in a few minutes the first turned and climbed back on the wood. That piqued my curiosity about man's language, though the two remained silent until we were several whale lengths from the white top. All the men on it jabbered and pointed their flippers as the other two swam the last few yards. Several smaller ships appeared on the horizon, headed towards the broken one, so I gave a great leap, slapped the water three times, and swam off.

That day I travelled under bright skies again, as if the typhoon had never happened. Sometimes, while I sunned in the lazy currents, letting birds pick sea-lice, or cruised the cool green aisles underwater, bouncing my song off the bottom, I thought I'd dreamed the whole thing. I added a passage to my song about the harpoon and the storm and the men. The part about the storm, I fancied, was the best: the waves came crashing about while Ohobo went striding across the sky.

Many thoughts came to me in the long solitary hours, and at night, under a full moon, my sleep was filled with dreams. In one of these a whale all of light rose up, gazed at me, and sank again out of sight. I felt a great longing to follow. I woke to find the moon low in the west, a pale shell before the rising sun.

I knew I was ready now to take The Plunge. The escape from the harpoon, the storm, the encounter with men, and the hours of solitude had made me ready. For three days I ate nothing. I swam along slowly, far from other creatures, ignoring the occasional gossipy bird.

Fasting changed things. For one, after the initial hunger passed, I felt lighter and stronger. I found it easier to concentrate, whether on a color of the ocean current, a thought, or a song. I felt both more inside myself and more keen at the edges. I at once felt detached from things and more *with* them. The world filled with an alert, sinewy peace.

I slept lightly those nights and the dream of the Whale of Light returned several times. The third night I hardly slept at all, singing my song over and over. That morning at sunrise I would take The Plunge.

When the first ray touched the whitecaps pink, I drew deep breaths, flooding my lungs and heart with air. After a last look at the sun, I heaved myself up and over and, with one strong twitch of my flukes, dove. Down I plunged through the green, the blue, into the black deep. Darker and darker it grew, colder and colder. Unafraid, I continued downward, past the luminary fish swimming in constellations through the black space of sea, down till they faded above me to the merest pinpoints of light, down into total darkness. Still I sank, feeling the terrible pressure crush me on all sides, feeling much like a stone. Still I knew no fear and I sang my song within me.

After a long time something rose under me and held me up like my mother. It was a second or two before I realized I'd touched bottom. I lay there for a long while, barely aware of time, of the ocean, of anything. I'd grown used to the pressure by now. The blood crept through my heart, lungs, and brain. The only noises were my heart beating—slowly, very slowly—and the swish of blood through my veins.

There I lay till I no longer noticed my heartbeat. I

noticed nothing, suspended in darkness. All thought had gone, even the sense of myself. The deep quiet became an alert and living substance that I was spread out in.

The rest is difficult to tell. But I shall try, even though I fail.

I felt I was where I should be, where I had always wanted to be. The past was not there, nor the future. There was only the present, infinitely full. Rather, the past was there as a small picture in my mind, to look at and enjoy, and also the future—something to look at and delight in, but not really there. All reality was in the present. The sense of want, of wanting to be back in the past or wanting to be ahead in the future, was gone. The sense of *want* was gone, because the want was filled in this darkness. I felt totally free, as if I were expanding through the darkness.

Suddenly, right at the center—of my heart, perhaps—there shone a tiny seed-pearl of light. It was a light that shone on my inner eye, so bright I couldn't focus on it. It grew and grew until it shone like a sun and swallowed up the darkness. And even though bright, it was soft; its radiance ceased to hurt my inner eye and I looked about with delight. I was swimming in a sea of light.

I remembered the tales of the Ocean of Light and felt—not afraid—but ashamed and a little silly for being there. Only then did I notice the singing. A low hum surrounded me. Whether it came through that light or was that light, I cannot tell. All I know is that I could now focus upon the light and see it moving even while it remained still. Then it became one long, low indescribable sound. I started to weep—really weep. I could feel the oil flow from my eyes as the sound drew forth tears.

And then, in the midst of the light, an even greater Light appeared, a flaming Light too great to look upon, in the shape of the whale of my dream. The whale drew closer and I knew I would be burned, but I didn't care, for I felt I would gladly die if only I could approach that Light. The Light sang to me, a voice musical and soft, and the words took shape in my head.

I saw my mother and father swimming together, with the light moving between them. Then I saw a tiny light in my mother and I knew it was me and I heard the Whale of Light sing louder—a note in a peculiar tone I'd never heard before, but recognized as *myself*. My heart leapt and I started to sing with him.

I saw myself grow in my mother's belly and be born, and I saw how her song became part of mine. I saw Lewtë flash across the shallows as her song wove itself with mine, and then the deep bass of my father joined us and made a chorus. As we swam to the polar seas Caloon's funeral made a note, and the romp with the sea lions made light grace notes, and so with every experience up to the present: each became part of the music. My brush with the whalers made a harsh note that nevertheless blent in, and the waterspout and typhoon a ponderous and majestic phrase. The note when I rescued the whalers sounded soft and sweet and was the most beautiful of all.

The Whale of Light stopped singing and turned to face me. Somehow I could look upon that Brightness without burning. His face had the most beautiful smile on it and even something of laughter, as if he found humor in all this. He showed me the future—not what would happen, but what I was meant to be. It was all tied in with what Hralekana had said, but mostly it was like that musical note sung at my conception. He showed me things I cannot express, things impossible to put into words.

All at once he turned and swam away in sport, beckoning me to follow. I chased after him, almost catching him, but never quite; he would dart away laughing, and I would chase after again. He would leap and I would leap, and at each leap I grew larger and stronger—though he always grew larger and stronger too.

At last we rested, and I looked full into his face and felt such love as I had never known, not even for my own mother and father. And I asked, "Are you the Spouter of Oceans?" He smiled and the smile grew infinitely wide and bright, and the brightness moved into me and wrapped me around, and I saw *that* before which all words drop away.

At length the light faded and I floated in a dark

peace lit by a faint glow. How long I rested in darkness I do not know, but it was a long time. Finally my lungs told me they needed air, and I rose slowly—almost floated up—past the dim galaxies of fish. I surfaced in the middle of the night. The moon was half-nibbled away and I lay there breathing softly. Never had air tasted so sweet and never had waves appeared more beautiful as from each of them flashed sparks from the Sea of Light.

Six

For several days I lay about, feeding on plankton and reflecting on my experience. I had taken The Plunge, and what I had learned would ever after guide me. I was in no hurry to be off. I lay there content to gaze upon sea and sky by the hour. It was the third day before I resumed my Cruise.

The waters were slightly cooler now and I swam fast and far. One morning I spied the decks of a ship on the horizon, glowing pink in the sun. I approached cautiously underwater, following the *thrug thrug* of the propeller. The ship was big—almost as big as the large whaling ship—but had many more eyes and was crowded up front with men. I surfaced a moment by its side. But I'd come too close. Submerging, I was sucked along the hull by the propellers. *Thrug thrug thrug*, the sound swelled as I slid helplessly back toward the whirling blades. With all my might I fought the current, but it was no use. Slowly, fathom by fathom, I was sucked down and back. *Thrug thrug thrug*, the giant propellers spun by, narrowly missing my flukes.

Then I was in the ship's wash, tumbling about like a calf. Soon I righted myself and came up gasping. It was not harpoons alone we had to fear from ships! I shuddered at the near miss and glanced at the ship's stern. No one was on deck but one of their young—still a calf, by its size. All the other men were forward. I'd glimpsed them looking out to sea through black things fastened to both eyes. This one calf lay under a lot of things shaped like giant clams and colored like sea anemones. Seeing me, he jumped up and made a noise. He ran to one of the colored things and took something green and red from under it (it looked half his size) and threw it over the rail. Curious, I followed it down. Whatever it was smelled like one of the islands at night. Gingerly I took it in my mouth and squeezed. Never before or since have I had a taste like that. It was sweet as an island breeze, that's all I can say. I breached the surface and turned a complete somersault. My friend was jumping up and down making noises, and others were running to join him; so I turned tail and dove.

That was my last contact with man for almost a year. The days grew longer. I yearned for the great beds of krill; so, continuing to follow the sun, I angled my way toward the end of the world, where I fed to my heart's content. I had many adventures that year, but they were all with the peoples of the sea. One of the less pleasant occurred as I was munching my way through krill and accidentally nipped the fluke of a giant Blue feeding across my path. With a roar the sea rose under me and I spat out a mouthful of shrimp. For

72

a moment I was marooned across a giant blue back. I lurched off forward, apologizing profusely, before the surprised Blue saw me.

But for the most part my encounters with other peoples were good. I came to know several other Blue whales—immense creatures with sulfur-colored bellies. Their kind had been hunted cruelly and few remained. There were more Fin and Sei whales about, whose larger numbers now bore the brunt of man's attacks. Sometimes I swam with pods of these for days on end.

That year in the icy waters I saw no other Humpbacks, a fact that worried me. But another part of me rejoiced to swim at the end of the world, far from my own kind, among strangers who taught me the thousand mysteries of the sea. I made friends with walruses, sea lions, elephant seals, and an albatross, Ala, who traveled with me through the mountains of ice.

We met one day when he—a mere speck high in the heavens—circled down to land on my back. I watched him come, fascinated by how large he loomed as he spiralled down. His body was white and his wings dark, stretching wide and motionless till he folded them.

"Whalers!" he cried, bending over to look in my eye upside down. "Whalers to starboard five leagues, and closing fast!" The pod of Sei whales and I thanked him and we all fled into the ice field.

These mountains were even vaster underneath the

water and, rubbing against each other, growled, roared, thundered and groaned, making a fearsome din. One night in the moon, under a light wind, they rang with a slight vibration, modulated in pitch and infinitely various. I was transfixed, listening to their singing, and Ala was too, perched like a bird of ice on top of an icy pinnacle.

Such was the beginning of a great friendship. I developed a real affection for my pert friend. And thanks to Ala, none of us saw a whaler that whole season. One day, watching me leap, Ala declared, "Humpbacks with their white wings are the birds of the sea."

I returned the compliment. "The Albatross," I said, "is clearly the whale of the air." And I meant it, for his wingspread stretched nearly three fathoms.

When the time came, I bade Ala farewell and swam back to warmer waters, always following the sun. I began to feel a bit lonely in my travels and strangely restless. For one thing I had not seen my pod, and one night woke terrified from a dream, calling Lewtë's name. I dreamt she had been harpooned. I heard her cry out in distress, and in the future that cry haunted my dreams.

But I was also curious to see more of the world. Remembering the men I'd rescued the year before and the one I'd seen on the stern of a ship, together with all the stories I'd heard of this strange land creature who hunted on the waters, I decided to find the coast where he lived and learn more about him for myself. I knew it was a dangerous desire, but gradually it became an obsession. I asked everyone I met, including dolphins, for news of that city of men where sea creatures were kept captive and where the Fin whale had been towed.

As before, the dolphins were the most helpful. They gave me elaborate directions. After several months' swimming I found myself traveling up a long coast crowded with mountains. I didn't see any men on the shore, but then I was too far away. I did pass a number of small boats, some driven by wind, some that churned noisily through the water. Once I came upon men swimming with large flippers attached to their small ones. They chased me, but I easily outswam them. I was careful to stay farther out after that.

One morning I surfaced to witness three ships heading toward the land, each pushed by smaller boats. The ships disappeared between two mountains. Swimming closer, I saw they had entered a narrow bay that reached back between the mountains. And then I stopped in mid-stroke.

Within the bay, spread up the sides of several mountains, lay the home of man. Yellow, pink, blue, and white, it shone like a coral reef of countless colors— only thousands of times larger. Everywhere its giant eyes gleamed in the morning light. Miles from it, I could see how it dwarfed the giant ships. I knew few whales would believe how enormous it was. Many ships were steering out of, as well as into, the bay. I was nearly run down by one before coming to myself. Shuddering, I fluked and resolved to wait for night for a closer look.

Meanwhile I cruised under a cliff that fell directly into the sea. The water was cool and shaded and I was settling down to a nap, my blowhole barely above the surface, when something landed on my back and began scrambling around. I snorted and surfaced. *Splash,* the intruder landed near my eye and came up bobbing. It had a face somewhat like a seal's, except furrier, and two finlike projections I guessed were ears.

"Sorry—mistook you for a rock—eh?" the interloper sputtered and disappeared, rising a few seconds later holding a mussel. As nonchalantly as if he were alone, the creature floated on his back by my eye. I counted four flippers, front and back. Reaching over to the cliff with one, he took a small rock and balanced it on his belly. Continuing to mutter, rapidly twitching his nose, he cracked open the mussel, gulped the insides, and flicked the empty shell over my back.

"What in Ocean *are* you?" I spouted. It was not a polite question, but the best I could offer after the rude interruption of my sleep.

He looked at me wide-eyed. "A sea otter, of course! Where have *you* been—eh?"

I don't think he meant this as an honest question, but with a loud snort I cleared my blowhole. "Around the world, several times," I replied, stretching the

76

truth a point. Meanwhile he dove again and was cracking open a second mussel, proceeding to chew noisily. Irritated, I asked in as civil a tone as I could manage, "Can you tell me about the city?"

He stared at me as if I'd lost my flippers. "Great Beds of Oysters, why?"

"I'd like to visit it."

He shook his head violently to clear the water from his ears and sneezed. "The water's terrible around the city and there are no fish. It's a rotten place for a sea otter. Why, I had a cousin—say, you wouldn't be one of those dolphins they keep in the lagoon, would you?"

I snorted so loud he jumped up on the rocks. "Of course not—course not—much too big, eh?" he chattered, his eyes and head darting about quickly. The whole time I was with him, he never remained still—a most unnerving creature. That must have been the result of living so close to man.

I asked him about the lagoon—where I could find it and what was there. He had seen it once, he said. It was filled with dolphins mostly, except—oh yes—for a whale even larger than myself. Lately he'd seen the ships tow in more captives—he couldn't be sure what kind. He dared not go too close.

Anyway, the city smelled worse than a beach of dead fish. And man was dangerous. He himself would never live closer to man. Many of his ancestors had been killed by them. In recent years it had been peaceful here outside the bay—except when two of his great-aunt's pups were captured alive.

Beyond that, he could tell me nothing, but kept twitching his whiskers at the notion I wanted to enter the bay. "You wouldn't catch *me* going there. No, not Okachi, eh?" He picked up another stone and put it down. What an agile animal, I thought. With some hesitation I asked him if he would pick a couple of barnacles off my nose, which had been itching for months. He obliged, and then with a shout slid down my side into the water. In a second he was up on the rocks and onto my back again, whirling as he slid toward my tail. He kept up this sport for a while, sliding and slithering, chattering and splashing. The bony tips of his little feet made first-rate back scratchers.

At last Okachi and I parted, friendly on both sides. I submerged for forty winks. Okachi had hardly dampened my enthusiasm for the city and I badly wanted to see more of it. I fell asleep thinking about the lagoon. At nightfall I woke to find the mountains black against a flaming red sky. I swam over to the main channel.

"BOOEEEP!" a great bellow resounded through the water. I shot to the surface, jolted nearly out of my skin. The source of the noise was a large ship a half mile out, headed for port. Several smaller boats whistled back, chugging to meet it. I decided to follow the ship in—at a safe distance.

It looked familiar, though I was sure I'd never seen it before. Metal flippers stuck out from its sides. I was

78

swimming behind, searching my memory, when every inch of skin tingled. Had I really heard it? For a moment a weak groan had sounded under the propeller's *thrug thrug*. Or so I thought.

All of a sudden I recalled where I'd seen the ship—or, rather, heard about it. It matched the description of the one that captured the Fin whale. I swam closer but could see nothing through the propeller's foaming turbulence. There . . . and there again! Was that a whistle? I strained my ears . . . Nothing. But what I had heard just might have been the feeble cry of a whale. I couldn't be sure—there were so many noises around ships: propellers churning, waves slapping, the creaking and humming of ropes. But if it *was* my imagination, it had made me think for half a second I heard the cry of a distressed Humpback.

I surfaced to get my bearings. What I then saw pushed the disturbing sounds from my mind. Awash in a polar pink twilight was a sight beyond description. Even now the memory defies finding the right words. Spread before me farther than I could see, rising up the sides of many mountains, lay the city of man. In every color of the coral islands, bright as the fish of tropical lagoons, more numerous than the largest school of herring, burned the eyes of the city. Some of them moved; others were still or winking. These eyes—most of them—dwarfed men; I could see men's tiny shadows passing along the quays and docks. Things with eyes growled, sputtered, and crawled along corridors through the city. Men climbed in and out of these—countless men, more than there are tiny beasts on a coral reef.

And the noise! It was unbelievable. Propellers thrugged, ships bellowed, hatches clanged, gulls screamed, ropes groaned, creeping things sputtered and over all rose a low roar as of distant surf, caused by the mingling of hundreds and thousands of sounds from the far reaches of the city.

And the smells! First I noticed the smell of dead fish, then of the rainbow-maker—the bitter stuff that ships burned and left on the water—then strange and enticing smells that blew from heaps on the docks. I submerged again and swam closer, only to be nearly blinded by the filthy water, my eyes stinging from oil and sludge. I passed a large tunnel discharging cloudy water into the bay and had to surface, the stench was so bad. I saw gulls picking over heaps of things that man had dumped over a small cliff. These smelled dead too. I recalled Delphi the Dolphin's remarks about man and reflected sadly that any creature who fouled his own waters surely wouldn't live long in the ocean.

My blowhole barely out of the water, I cruised close to the docks as long as I could stand it—for miles and miles it seemed. By the time I remembered to look, the ship I'd followed was far across the bay, heading further inland. Night came quickly, veiling all except the city, which glowed more brightly in the dark. With a sinking feeling I hurried to catch up. The ship's lights went on, but other lights appeared on the far shore, and soon I could not tell its from the others.

Fortunately the ship had headed up the bay. That was where Okachi told me I would find the lagoon and the captive dolphins. Slowly, marveling at the lights of the city and fearful of running aground in the dark, I swam up the bay. I wonder if the Whale of Light aided my thoughts then, because I began to think what I'd never thought before. Such thoughts have come more frequently with the years.

"Man," I thought to myself, "is a strange creature. At night he is like those fish of the black deep who've learned to glow because they have no other light. Yet man has the sun by day and the moon and stars by night. Could it be that man's eyes don't see those lights well?" I concluded that of all creatures man is the greatest mystery, because one can never know for sure what he will do. At the time I couldn't know how prophetic this last thought was.

Seven

Lost in such reflections, I hardly noticed the cool dawn mist rising. A noisy bunch of gulls landed on my head and began pecking at barnacles. They were a scruffy-looking bunch. One had lost a leg. Scree, as he was called, hopped about, balancing himself with his wings. He was talkative, and informed me the gulls lived on what men threw into the ocean. More important, he revealed the lagoon was an hour's swim up the bay. But he never did say how he lost his leg.

While we talked, a small boat putted out of the fog, carrying two men. The mouth opened on one and a burning thing fell, hissing on the water. He made a sound, but the boat vanished again in the fog before the other man turned. I could hear the boat begin to circle back, though, so I fluked without saying good-bye.

When I surfaced again, the fog had parted and was rolling away up the land. The sight is fixed in my memory. The green land and pink mist stretched away to white-topped mountains—enormous waves of land higher than the highest in the sea. Rocks and tall plants shone in the early light and from them the land swept down to cliffs of many colors which fell steeply into the bay. Here and there the dwellings of men glinted in the sun among expanses of yellow, brown, and green plants which reminded me of kelp beds. The bay itself shone silver, stretching inland beyond sight.

Nevertheless, the view left me uneasy. A sense of anxiety had been growing in me all night, ever since I thought I heard whale cries. The beauty of the landscape made me feel a greater urgency to find the lagoon. What began as restless curiosity was now an obsession. Unaccountable feelings of panic and anger swept through me, and I had forcibly to resist them. I wondered if the polluted waters had affected my brain.

Even if another whale had been captured by the ship, I reasoned, it would do no good for me to get upset. Of course I knew I was taking a chance of getting caught myself, coming this close to man's habitat. It made me uneasy that the small boat had spotted me. But there was no immediate danger, and I prided myself on dismissing fanciful fears. I concluded the oil in the water was making me skittish.

At last I spied the lagoon—a small body of water set within the shore. Above it red, blue, and yellow flags fluttered as if from the masts of a ship. Beyond it rose a number of brightly colored human dwellings, and a deep inlet led to it. I submerged—the water was cleaner here and didn't hurt my eyes—and surfaced behind a cluster of rocks near the inlet.

On the far side of the lagoon hundreds of men, as gaily colored as tropical fish, were milling about. From a pool above the ground a dolphin would now and then leap straight into the air and knock a round red thing out of a man's flipper. The other men would roar at this and slap their flippers. Sometimes two sea lions climbed up, barked, and tossed the red thing back and forth before splashing into the pool. From another pool a black-and-white Killer whale lunged and took a fish from a man's flipper. Since no man was near the lagoon, I thought I'd swim over for a look.

Cautiously I approached the inlet, which was blocked by a net, much larger than those we found floating in the ocean. Sometimes fish were caught in these. I'd been warned that whales could get tangled in them and drown. I swam up slowly and nudged it gingerly; it was made of metal, not rope. It stretched from the bottom of the bay to several fathoms above the water. I followed its length, reaching from one side of the inlet to the other. There were no holes in it larger than a sea otter could squeeze through. I was beginning to inspect it all over again when two shapes darted up on the other side.

"Look, Marmo, it's a whale, and he's not tied to anything!" a blue dolphin exclaimed to a marbly blue-and-white one. The two pressed their thin noses through the squares of the net as I swam over to them. Silly dolphins that they were, they squeaked and wriggled from excitement.

"Who are you?" both asked at once.

I told them and asked if either knew Whitefin, the dolphin who had told me about the lagoon. Marmor shook his head vigorously. "My cousin! Yes, she's my cousin. She visited us here." The blue one agreed.

I told them I was here to learn more about man, and because I felt, well . . . compelled. I also wanted to find out what had become of the Fin whale.

"He's here! He's here!" they squeaked, rubbing their snouts together. "His name is Finuwë and he's supposed to surface each day in the middle of our act—the men grow all excited when he does—but mostly he just lies at the bottom and broods. Would you like to meet him?"

I said I would. But first, would they tell me more about their life here? Each kept interrupting the other in true dolphin fashion as they bubbled over with talk.

From their description it appeared that man, though deficient in certain qualities, was even more intelligent than anyone had suspected. The first thing they'd discovered was that man would feed them fish from his clever flippers whenever they leaped into the air or rolled over on the surface. Sometimes men would come swimming in the lagoon, and although they had a funny shape (like a frog's, if I'd ever seen any of those creatures), they showed signs of affection, both giving and receiving caresses.

Even more surprising, they never tried to bite or harm the dolphins and had not torn apart the Fin whale—as they did other whales on the high sea. I said maybe it was because these men were full and, like some other beasts, harmless when they weren't hungry. The dolphins thought this might explain it, because the men here had so many fish they shared them freely. In fact, men kept the Killer whale in the lagoon so fat he was really harmless and quite jovial.

A slight shudder travelled down my spine, as I'd heard stories of packs of these Killer whales attacking others. Yet the men here, most of whom were no larger than a gray seal, swam next to him unafraid while he teased and played with them. His name was Uton, and he ate a great deal.

When they finished I inquired if they were happy in the lagoon.

They looked down for a moment and the blue one, Scallop, replied, "It's rewarding to observe man's intelligence and attempt to learn his language. And perhaps, through us, he is learning how to get along better with other creatures. But he has not yet learned to let us come and go as we please. He keeps us and the others trapped behind this net."

"It's true," Marmo added, "we'd leave if we could, but men lower the net only to bring in new captives." His eyes brightened. "Say, did you follow in that whale who arrived yesterday?"

"What whale?" I asked, again feeling strangely uneasy.

"The one who arrived nearly dead from fear and weariness. It went to sleep and hasn't wakened yet. Wait a second; we'll get—"

They whistled off in mid-sentence into the murky

depths of the lagoon. Waiting there by the steel net, I felt more and more uneasy as the seconds passed. I wished both hadn't left.

Then I heard it—and couldn't believe I heard it—a low and pitiful moan, followed by a whistle. All at once I knew why I'd felt anxiety, dread, and a strange urgency throughout the night. My sixth sense had known all along—even when I was at the mouth of the bay and perhaps earlier. I could mistake that cry for no one else's in the world. It was Lewtë's.

"Lewtë!" I cried.

"Hrūna!" a weak voice returned and my heart dissolved. Without thinking I crashed into the steel cables, scraping my nose. But I didn't feel it. I saw two white flippers on the other side and then Lewtë and I were rubbing noses through the net and the water was murky with big oily tears. It was a while before either of us could speak.

In broken sobs she told me how one moonlit night the pod was sleeping near an island when men approached in a silent boat. Too late, Hrōta had whistled a warning. She felt a sting in her fin and blacked out. When she came to, she was tied to a ship thrugging through water miles away. She heard her parents cry out to her, following far off, but the ship was fast and soon she heard nothing but its propeller.

For seven days she couldn't eat because of the lump in her throat. She then decided she must eat to have strength to escape and swallowed some of the shrimp the men gave her. Frequently she cried out in distress, hoping another Humpback would hear and come to her aid. After weeks of this, she'd arrived here only yesterday.

Lewtë was twice as large as I remembered her, but with the same white streaks from flippers to flukes. Not only had she grown up, but she was beautiful. Beautiful and helpless! Man the monster had trapped her. I felt fire in my brain.

"Look out!" I cried, backing up, and rammed full speed into the net. The thing shuddered, but didn't give; a cable cut me sharply across the lip. Enraged, I battered the net again and again, crying out Lewtë's name.

"Stop!" she screamed until finally I heeded her. Blood was clouding my eyes. "Please stop! You've hurt yourself."

"It won't do any good," said a deep voice somewhere behind her. "I've tried." I strained to see through the clouded water. A dark shape moved up. It was the Fin. He was black, sleek, and still young, but had scars where he'd fought against man's ropes. He dwarfed Lewtë and was longer than I by the length of half my flipper. "We have to wait until men open the net—unless . . ." He paused and looked at me, a mysterious smile stretching along his jaw.

"Unless what?" I asked, still angry.

"Come and see." He moved off. "I've been working at it." On opposite sides, we swam to one end of the

91

net. There at the bottom, the thick cable holding the net to the man-made reef was nearly rusted through. It had been twisted and a number of the strands broken.

"I've been pushing against this, and it's giving, slowly," the Fin said. "Perhaps if we work from both sides it will go more quickly."

He didn't need to ask me twice.

"Be careful," Lewtë warned me through the net. "You're still bleeding."

The Fin and I went to work. Crash—first he hit the corner of the net, then—smash—I hit it from the opposite side. The net shook and roiled the surface; I wondered how long it would be before men noticed. Crash—then smash—and crash again.

Each blow hurt terribly and our blood mingled in the water, but slowly, strand by strand, the rusted cable gave. At last it snapped.

"Look out, Hrūna," the Fin shouted, and backing up, swam at the loose corner full speed. As he hit it, the steel net bent slightly out and up, leaving room for a dolphin to squeeze through. Marmo and Scallop, who were watching, shot past me. Liberated, they frisked joyfully about.

But others were watching too. Something silver shot through the water, narrowly missing my tail. I rolled and surfaced. Men stood on top of the reef, pointing something into the water. Several shouted and I ducked as a second flash buried itself in the bottom.

"Darts!" Lewtë cried. "Look out—they put you to

sleep." I backed away from the net, watching the surface. The Fin had widened the gap and was running at it again. With another blow he bent it wide enough for Lewtë to wriggle through. In a second she was at my side. Both of us scanned the surface for darts. Another flashed between Marmo and Scallop.

"Go!" we shouted at them.

"Goodbye," they whistled. "We'll see you again," and were off like darts themselves.

With a great bellow the Fin hit the net a last time and thrust through, scratching himself terribly on the rusty cable. Blood rose in a reddish stream from his side.

"Flee!" he cried, lunging toward us.

Zing, a dart sang between Lewtë and me. We turned tail and swam for our lives.

A mile out we surfaced. The shore was lined with men waving their flippers and pointing. While we rested, Lewtë inspected my cuts and the Fin's. None was serious, though we'd both bear scars to the end of our days. A sleek white-and-black shape flashed by, whistling thanks. It was Uton, the Killer whale, followed by a family of sea lions and a pod of porpoises. A minute later a white Beluga whale passed doing barrel rolls. Last of all a bulbous Manatee lumbered by, chewing kelp. By then three men had scrambled into a boat and were buzzing toward us. We fluked and swam hard down the bay, Lewtë and I side by side and flipper to flipper.

Eight

The first few miles we sped near the surface, rising often. My lips and forehead began to throb, but I didn't care. Lewtë was with me and that was all that mattered. Finuwë the Fin cruised silently beside us, lost in his own thoughts. The water grew murkier as we neared the city. Its stone pinnacles sparkled in the midday sun, but our eyes were elsewhere. All across the bay, coming toward us in a line, swam boats of every size—a few with high, white fins. Many of the smaller ones made a whining noise.

Lewtë turned, swimming nervously in a circle. "They're coming for us. They have the stinging darts!" she cried, her voice shaking.

"No matter," I said to calm her, "we'll just have to swim deep." But I knew the bay was shallow under the boats and that we'd be within range of the darts. I felt sick but dared not show it. The Fin's eyes gleamed as he took me aside. He whispered in my ear, outlining a plan.

I agreed to it, but had my doubts. Battering the lagoon net had cost nearly all my strength. Lewtë was weak and even the Fin showed signs of tiring. The line of ships suggested whalers to me. What if we had to swim under harpoons?

An explosion shook the water. We stared at each other. Four more followed in quick succession. They hurt our ears. Instinctively we turned back. "Wait a moment," cried the Fin. "What are we afraid of?"

"Harpoons," I replied.

"I would rather face a harpoon," he grunted fiercely, "than captivity again." Lewtë shivered and nodded. I knew they meant it and, recalling with a shudder the harpoon that nicked me, turned to face the oncoming fleet. We were silent. Lewtë and I gently slapped each other and nuzzled side by side a moment. Whatever happened would happen to us together.

So we three, spaced far enough apart to make separate targets, swam that blue morning toward we knew not what. More explosions shook the water—louder and at shorter intervals. We headed toward one side of the flotilla, hoping to slip under the smaller boats. If they had darts, we'd be easier targets on that side, but they were less likely to have harpoons.

Now we could see men lining the sides of the boats. As we surfaced a last time, one pointed and yelled. We plunged to the bottom racing toward them.

BOOM—BOOM—explosions rocked us. Head throbbing, I pressed my tongue against the roof of my mouth and kept on. Over us loomed dark bottoms and white wakes. As we passed under them, an enormous explosion hit one side, but we saw no harpoon. I suspect the sound was meant to drive us to the surface.

Once on the far side of the boats, Finuwë and I told

98

Lewtë to go on ahead. Then, according to plan, we swam back up behind the boats. At the Fin's whistle we rose, each heaving his flukes out of the water, lifting a boat high and dumping its crew. I caught sight of a man in another boat aiming a long tube at me. I heard a sharp crack as something stung my fin.

"A dart!" I cried out, my heart cold as a fish. I plunged after Lewtë.

"My fin—it's been struck by a dart."

She examined my fin and found a little blood trailing from it, but no dart. Whatever it was had gone in one side and out the other. Lewtë started to cry, but I was relieved.

"It's nothing to worry about," I reassured her, as Finuwë joined us and we left the boats behind, speeding into the dirty waters near the bay's entrance. I never thought I'd love polluted waters, but in those murky depths we could hide from pursuers.

We stayed under as long and as deep as possible, coming up only twice for air near rocky cliffs, where we were less likely to be noticed. Several times we heard something noisy pass overhead in the air. After it passed twice I risked rising to have a peek. In a second it was over me. The noise was deafening.

I hurried back to the bottom.

"What is it?" the others asked.

"I don't know. Another man-thing. It flies in the air like a bird and can hover in one place. Its wings make a sound like thunder." We hugged the bottom, swimming from rock to rock. The thunderwing continued to pass over. When its sound grew faint I surfaced again and looked behind. The boats that had tried to block our escape had turned and were coming after us. And they were gaining.

"We'll have to swim for it down the main channel," I told the others. We did, glad that it deepened slightly toward the open sea. Yet we had still to pass the narrows at the mouth of the bay. Occasionally we heard an explosion in the distance, but they were less frequent now. The main channel was straight and easy to observe. Fortunately even out there man's pollution had clouded it. All of us were black on top, except for our flippers, and we just might pass unobserved. I wondered how the other escapees were doing, especially the white Beluga and the dolphins.

Soon the water tasted sweeter and looked clearer. The bottom dropped below us and the huge shoulders of the narrows loomed up on either side.

"It's not far now," the Fin whispered and we bent our flukes with a will. We heard the thunderwing pass once more at a distance. The shoulders of the mountains shrank back. Blue water smiled at us.

Lewtë and I started to sing, but the Fin cut us short.

"Look up there," he whispered. Far above, something white bobbed at the surface. Its shape was familiar. We rose. A lump swelled in my throat—it was Marmo, floating dead.

None of us spoke a word as we stared at the still

body of our friend rocking stiffly in the waves. At last the Fin choked out, "Let's go."

"Wait!" cried Lewtë, who had swum close. "There's a dart in his side. He's not dead, only asleep."

Sure enough, the dart was there—and a rope around his tail attached to a red floating ball, though no boat was near and no man.

"The thunderwing," I guessed out loud. "The thunderwing did this."

We nudged Marmo, but he did not respond. Lewtë managed with her flipper to dislodge the dart and while we held the dolphin between us, the Fin tugged at the red ball until the rope slipped off, taking a patch of skin with it. Marmo groaned a little.

Intent on our work, we didn't hear the boat approach. A shot cracked and a dart skipped inches from my nose. I turned to see a thin boat skimming the waves toward us. A second dart narrowly missed Lewtë's dorsal. In one motion we plunged to the blue deep. We lay there, angrily twitching our flippers, watching the boat far above move slowly toward the helpless Marmo. Finuwë and I exchanged glances. When the boat stopped, we rose toward it.

Together our foreheads struck the keel and lifted it far out of the water. Three men spilled into the brine, shouting. Ignoring them we turned to Marmo, who groaned and twitched his flukes. We pushed him far from the boat, shouting at him, trying to bring him to. Far off, we could hear the thunderwing approaching.

"Dive, Marmo!" we yelled. "Dive for your life!"

With a sharp cluck, he opened both eyes. "Where . . . ?" he murmured.

"Dive!" we shouted once more, and he did, a bit wobbly. Just in time, too, as the thunderwing was over us.

At the bottom Lewtë scrutinized him carefully. Aside from a small puncture, Marmo was all right; he thanked us profusely over and over as we swam out ever deeper.

When Marmo had come to completely, the Fin said, "We'd better go our separate ways, in case we're followed." We agreed to meet next season at the end of the world. After what we'd been through in the past hours, none could speak another word. We nuzzled a moment and then, without looking back, headed in different directions into the open sea. All except Lewtë and I, that is, who chose the same course. We two cruised off, flipper to flipper. Without saying a word, we knew we would never again part.

All that day we swam silently into the blue sea. And that night, under a crescent moon glittering on the white hair of the waves, we wreathed our spouts together in a single fountain of breath—the sign from ages beyond memory that a bull and cow henceforth joined their lives. We would swim the same seas, eat the same krill, birth the same calves, and grow old together until one, and then the other, passed through the deep into the Ocean of Light.

No one observed the ritual except two terns, who flew in a circle above us, singing. After the Spouting, we swam, threading our songs together for the first time. Neither had heard the other's song and both songs had grown over the past year.

Even now I can hear our wedding song as we wove it around the waves, the flying spindrift, and the shy yellow light of the moon. Never have I heard a cry more beautiful than Lewtë's. Her high yearning voice probed like moonlight into the pearl caverns of the sea. Then I heard my own voice respond. It was my voice and my song all right, but I felt as if someone else were singing. I did not need to think; the notes, always before released in solitude, wove themselves effortlessly around Lewtë's plaintive cries.

Throughout that night the moonlit canyons of the sea echoed and re-echoed to the song of our love. The song began with our birth, our gazing at each other from the great safe islands of our mothers, and the tentative first greetings and shy fleeings. It continued with our growing friendship, our romping together and mischievous diving over the backs of the sleeping elders. It included the trip to the end of the world and the self-conscious shyness of adolescence—those long solitary times when we thought we sang to no one, yet in reality sang to each other.

My song included adventures with my father, the meeting with Hralekana, the Plunge, the near-harpooning, and the storm; and Lewtë's, her adventures on the Lonely Cruise, her counsel by the Father of Whales, her vision in the Deep, and the terrifying ordeal of her capture. (Her voice grew urgent and dissonant at this point.) Our song climaxed with the tale of our meeting at the lagoon and stormy escape, but did not end there.

It continued in a softer vein, taking up our yearning, the wreathing of our breath and the yellow moonlight on the waves. We sang of the present—this moment of our love's realization—while the song spread back over the past and into the future and had no ending. And then there was no past and no future and only this Now in which we sang on and on. And in the pauses of our singing we heard what is not vouchsafed to every whale to hear, and which at first we thought we only imagined—the distant, elusive chorus of the mermaids, returning our song from the edge of the world.

In awe we heard what inspired our greatest singer to intone,

> Sweet waves, run softly till we end our song
> Upon this bridal day, which is not long.
> For we of joy and pleasance to you sing
> That all the waves may answer and our echo ring.

Their voices swelled from the waves, wild and sweet, suspending us in sound, and we knew now the siren song that had called many a whale recklessly over the seas to perish on rocks or be stranded on shore.

But for us their song, however sweet, held no peril, for it was the echo of our love, of all our joy in the present, now and forever complete. We were one, not as two halves are one, but rather as two selves become a greater one—while all things sang around us, moving about us, circle within circle, forever at the center of the dance.

Slowly and shyly we began to act out the dance, slapping the water with our flippers, gently at first, then louder and louder till the sound resounded for miles. Gently, we nuzzled and slapped each other, turning away, back to back, and diving in opposite directions down into the black deep, there crying our songs and feeling for each other. We came together, flipper to flipper, heads up, speeding toward the surface. Louder we sang until the moon waffled above us through the water and with a loud cry we breached the surface, still clinging to each other, nine fathoms into the air, to crash breathless on our backs.

We paused for a blessed moment, and slowly, gently, slapped the water again, and so down again and up under the witnessing moon until the moon tired and grew pale and lifted its flukes in the west. We fell asleep in an enormous bed of kelp, the voices still ringing in our ears.

Sweet waves, run softly till we end our song . . .

So began a month of our lives that now seems outside the tides of the sea. For this long honeymoon we swam slowly to warmer waters, staring in wonder at the blue sky, the dancing waves, and the ever-varying gold of the sun on the ocean floor, over which cruised our shadows side by side. One night we surfaced by a tropical island; the aroma from its fruit and flowers hung over the sea. We lay there breathing it in. Midway through the night points of fire appeared on the shore. More followed until they dimly lit the shapes of men getting into narrow boats. The men paddled out into the lagoon (we were safely beyond the reef) and began to spear fish. Each boat bore a torch and a spearman, and the reflection from all the torches danced upon the lagoon's surface among the cold sparks of moonlight. Others, perhaps the females, danced upon the shore, singing and making loud noises with sticks. It was a different sort of singing, short-breathed and abrupt, and yet it moved us to see men do something so beautiful. Lewtë snuggled under my flipper, the far torches sparkling in her eyes, and we rolled round and round in time to the distant drums.

Nine

Not long after that we met the Manatee again, puffing and snorting his slow way along, trailing a streamer of kelp. He hid his face while shyly thanking us between bites of kelp and said he hoped to reach his native coast in a few months. He thought rations were sparse on the open sea for a vegetarian like himself and had taken the precaution of bringing his own along. Then he grew too shy altogether, wrapped himself in the kelp, and slowly waggled off.

When the moon was again in the crescent, we started out for the end of the world with the vague hope of running across our pod. On our way we skirted land again, this time a coast of snow-topped mountains. At first we stayed far out. But now and then we spied a thin white streak falling down a cliff into the sea. Curious, we swam closer to investigate. It was water falling from the snows and made a thunderous noise where it struck the ocean, stirring up the warmer brine with cold currents.

I wanted to stay away from it, remembering vividly our recent escape. But Lewtë coaxed and wheedled, and at last plunged recklessly under it. Little by little I edged in after her, until we rolled together in the foaming torrent. It was wonderful! It teased, tickled, and rubbed us all over. Even better, if we surfaced and took the full force of the fall, it scrubbed the barnacles off our backs. We spent two days by these cataracts till we were picked smooth as newborn calves.

We reached the great beds of krill without seeing any kin, though we both ran across old friends. Ala became our constant companion, together with a smaller, even whiter albatross, whom he introduced as Ali.

As before, they kept watch for whaling fleets, and in turn our backs provided them with a warm perch above the water. We also were able to help them in a tight spot. One moonlit night, while they were off hunting, the fog closed in, covering the ice, the ocean, and ourselves. The two of them, tireless flyers, dared not descend among the ice mountains for fear of colliding with one in the fog. Lewtë and I woke to hear their cries far above us. We began to slap the water loudly, keeping it up until the sound and its echoes guided the two safely down to our backs. They were extremely grateful, for though albatrosses can glide for hours, the two were near the end of their strength.

Ala and Ali stayed with us until the day they left for their nesting grounds. That year we also met our friend the Fin and schools of dolphins who told us the story of our escape as Marmo and Scallop had related it to the whole dolphin kingdom. It was stretched in a few places, but was recognizably the same tale. The dolphins showered us with fish—a new experience for Lewtë.

Ala and Ali had been gone months when they surprised us one morning flying low over the water. Behind them, flapping its wings to catch up, hurried a fledgling, the down still covering its new feathers. From the way they circled it, and the absurd expression of pride on their faces, we guessed this awkward young flying machine belonged to them. Gray and fuzzy, it had ridiculously large feet and beak. I submerged to hide the smile curling all the way to my flippers.

As I rose the whole family alighted on my back—the youngest with a clunk and a squawk. Ala, stretching his wings their full seventeen feet, announced, "Hrūna, we'd like you to meet the newest addition to our family—Ross."

"Hello, Ross," I spouted, in what I thought was an avuncular tone. Ross honked, hid his head under his wing, and tripped over his left foot. Mother and Father had to lift him up. Lewtë was swimming round and round in an admiring way, and soon she and Ali were fast in a conversation about hatching and calving.

Albatrosses usually hatch only one baby and, like whales, make a great fuss over their accomplishment. Soon Ala was busy teaching Ross to pluck barnacles off my back. The tyke managed to knock one off, then missed and gouged my skin. He fell down three times before his parents and he flew off to an ice floe. Ross did better in the air than on my back, because his wings already had some of the albatross spread. His parents could glide for hours without effort, appearing to sleep on the wing.

It was a pleasure to have my old friend and his family back. Lewtë and I would scoop up krill while the three hung above us, picking from what we brought to the surface. Where the krill were too spread out, we'd swim in ever-tightening circles, spouting bubbles to crowd them to a ball at the surface. Then we had to be especially careful not to close our mouths over Junior, who often sat down to feed right on the mass of shrimp.

One misty morning I was wakened by Ali's shriek, "Hrūna! Hrūna! Come quick. It's Ross." I plunged toward her, breaking out of the mist. There I saw an alarming sight. Ala was rapidly circling a small ice floe, screaming and diving at the waves. The floe was rocking as something bumped it from below. A moment later I caught sight of three shark fins. Perched on the floe was Ross, his wings extended, opening and shutting his mouth. He was too panicked to fly and the sharks were about to capsize the ice in their effort to get at him. They were breaking off chunks of it. The largest shark heaved half his length up one side, wildly snapping his jaws. The floe tilted and Ross slid toward the razor-sharp teeth.

Bellowing, I charged. Two sharks heard me coming and fled, but my flukes caught the largest, his head still on the ice, and sent him flying. At the blow the ice nearly flipped, but the sudden movement launched Ross into the air, where at last he found his wings.

Ala and Ali were overjoyed and swung in great circles around him. The youngster had learned a new lesson about the sky being the safest place for a bird.

A second season passed at the end of the world without sight of our pod, though the dolphins assured us they were all right. One morning, just about the time we became restless for warmer waters, Lewtë woke me with a new, soft note in her song. The past several weeks she'd spent in the krill beds, stuffing herself in preparation for the long trip—overdoing it a bit, I thought. Now she swam up to me with a shy smile and nudged me with her flipper. All at once I understood the new note.

I grew excited and leaped so high I rid myself of a season's barnacles. It took me a while to calm down, even though I knew Lewtë would be carrying our calf more than a year. I swam in rapid circles around her, suddenly worried about Killer whales and sharks, though none was near. She laughed at me, but that day and the day after I stayed right by her side in the krill beds to prevent anyone's bumping into her.

The third morning we left for warmer waters. We swam slowly, resting where we found food. I was anxious now to locate a pod of Humpbacks—our own, I hoped—for Lewtë needed more protection.

One night we thought we heard a snatch of Humpback song. It faded just as quickly as it came from the canyon beneath us. We thought we'd dreamed it, for the desire for our own kind was strong upon us. Gone for two years now, we wondered if any of them would recognize us.

In the morning we followed the sea canyon, hoping to hear the song again. The sky was overcast, and for the first time together, we felt a little lonely. We didn't feel much like singing, but decided we'd better try. So we sang our blended songs and then were quiet, listening. In a few minutes we heard a faint medley of voices sounding vaguely familiar. We leaped forward toward the gray horizon.

We swam half the day. We were beginning to tire, though we grew more excited as the voices drew closer. Finally we made out black shapes on the horizon, surrounded by white water. Together we leaped high. Four leaped in response. A short while later we recognized the faces of our parents, Hreelëa and Hrunta and Waleena and Krala, coming joyfully toward us.

Never in my life had I heard such a chorus of snorts, whistles, bellows, sputterings, trumpetings, trillings, snufflings, and gruntings. And the slapping—it was deafening! We smacked the water as we nuzzled with our parents, while the other whales gathered in a circle, waiting to welcome us. Calves skipped and cavorted on the outside, but I didn't recognize any of these youngsters. I noticed that those who were calves when I left were now half-grown, and calves Lewtë and I had played with were enormous—full-grown, or almost so.

It made me feel small.

Hreelëa was nuzzling us both, making little trilling sounds, when Hrunta drew back and stared at me.

"It is even as Hralekana said," he announced, his eyes shining. "You are not only larger than I, but among the biggest of Humpbacks." That surprised me; I glanced at either flipper and bent my tail to look at it. It *did* stretch back a way and my flukes (which I'd always admired) *were* huge. But while hanging about Fins and Blues I hadn't thought so. The blood rushed to my head and I suppressed a grin.

We all nuzzled and rolled over many times. Then began the games I remembered so well from the time the fathers had returned. The adults leaped over and over each other, braiding long wakes down which the calves skidded and rolled. The sun came out as we frolicked, the sea for miles resounding to our slaps and the thunder of whale after whale leaping free of the water, white flippers flashing like wings. While we leapt we sang, first the Song of the Pod, then the Song of the Hunt, the Song of the Sun and Moon, and the Song of the Lonely Cruise. After these we sang the Song of the Cow and Bull, the Song of the Calf, and the Song of the Pod again. The Song of the Sun and Moon was my favorite, for it told of the swimming of those two great bodies through the sky:

115

SONG OF THE SUN AND MOON

High in the black heavens where a million herring
Shine as they turn and swim over the sea,
Up leaps the White Cow, lovely and lingering,
Her milk meandering the mouth of each wave.
Then like a fire from the farthest fathom
Bursts the Red Bull, her beauty pursuing,
The heat of his love the high heaven filling
Until his flukes flash and he falls in the deep.
So the White Cow, widening and withering,
Lures the Red Bull to leap after her love:
Now do her fair flukes fling far their glory—
Now does his dayspring dwindle the darkness.

At the end of the day, exhausted from our reunion, the pod huddled in a circle around the calves and, flipper to flipper, tails in the air, slept utterly content.

The next day we shared the tale of the past two years. There was much marveling over Lewtë's escape from the lagoon. The pod had mourned her capture for days. I still had a scar from battering the steel net, which attracted more credit than it deserved. Afterwards we heard the pod's story. They had thriven both years, meeting no whalers at the end of the world.

Finally, they explained an absence we'd noticed, but which no one mentioned until now. Hrōta, old and weary, had at last joined his mate in the Ocean of Light. One day he told them his time had come, bade farewell, and swam off alone singing his death song. At some unknown spot he had breathed his last, surrendered himself to the black deep, and ascended into that Ocean that knows no tide. My father now led the pod.

Our stories occupied the whole day. Toward sundown my father beckoned to me to swim off with him, as in the old days. When the plunging sun lifted his flukes lighting the sky rose-red, Hrunta turned to me. "Hrōta's last wish was that if you ever returned—and he was certain you would—you were to lead the pod."

I didn't know what to say. Dismayed, I protested I wasn't old enough and knew nothing about leading. Besides, wasn't he, Hrunta, the new leader?

My father smiled. "That may be true, son, but I have only been holding the position for you. Never fear! You will not lead without my guidance or that of the elders. Hrōta saw that you had the mark of a leader, and Hralekana confirmed it."

We swam back, but I kept the secret from Lewtë until the Council of Elders announced it.

So began a period of intense training to which I gave all my daylight hours. The Council took me into their confidence and instructed me of the winds and tides, the waters safest for calving, the movement of the great beds of krill, the channels of underwater communication, the means of defense, celestial navigation, and the laws of the pod. They described man's depredations upon the Humpbacks and the places to go to avoid him. Always and ever they impressed upon me that, as leader, the greatest responsibility was mine, that I would be first to face danger and last to flee it, but that as I did so, I could count on the support of the pod.

Then, just before the calving, six of us left for the end of the world to locate the beds of krill for the next polar season. An elder, four others, and I went, three of them from my own year. The trip was successful and without mishap, though I'd never travelled so long a distance in so short a time. I was glad to return to Lewtë, who was swelling in girth though she wasn't due for a year. The rest of that lazy warm-water season we lolled about the islands, renewing old friendships, playing with the new calves, and getting to know the pod which I would lead on its annual migration.

Ten

So it was that after a few months had passed and the calves were old enough to swim a long distance, I led the pod into colder waters and the most perilous adventure of our lives. Everyone had eaten as much as possible in the past weeks, knowing there would be little food on the journey, and little time to eat it, until the thousands of miles were passed that lay between us and the end of the world.

To this day I remember my feeling of pride as I set out at the head of the pod under a shrimp-pink sunrise. Lewtë, heavier now, and a bit ungainly, swam at my side with a pleased look. Four or five gulls circled us, shrieking. All together we trumpeted our Going Forth Song and listened while its thousand echoes rolled back to us from the canyons over which we'd pass.

The calves sported at first, then settled down to serious swimming. I was apprehensive that first day, as Lewtë and the other pregnant cows could not maneuver very fast. I kept a sharp eye out for Killer whales. Harmless enough as individuals, in groups Killer whales—especially when hungry—were dangerous to a straggler.

The day came and went without incident; so did that week, and the next, and the next. We met dolphins halfway, who informed us the Manatee had finally reached his oriental shore. Further, they said the only whaling fleets sighted in cold waters were half-way around the world. Much to our delight, on that voyage we encountered the same tribe of sea lions my father had helped long ago. Leading them, even more hoary about the nose, was Siloa. We took a day off from travel to spend with that frolicsome crowd.

Though leading the pod soon became routine, I felt a vague uneasiness, which I put down to the newness of it all. I resolved to put it out of my mind. There was too much to enjoy. At these latitudes the stars shone brighter and closer to us. Each night I would measure our journey by the constellation of the Leaping Whale, which rose ever higher over the horizon. Even in daytime, when its jewellike flukes were hidden by the sun, I steered the pod toward it.

One night we were struck by a violent storm and had to sleep at the bottom, snuggling with the calves and teaching them to laugh at Ohobo and his harpoon, which lit all the surface above us.

Soon the increased vigor from cold water and the sight of our frosty spouts told us—if the height of the Leaping Whale didn't—that we were only days from our summer feeding grounds. Lewtë had made the trip well, losing little weight; still, she was hungry for the luscious krill. We swam faster those two days, from daybreak until stars glowed over us like phosphorous fish. Early next morning I spouted in joy as we passed the first iceberg—a small one, but a sign we were near journey's end.

A chorus of squeals rose when we sighted the krill that afternoon. With a flash of her flippers, Lewtë left my side and made a wide hole in that wilderness of shrimp. We fed all that day and the next and, as usual, overdid it. We should have known better. The second night we all felt water-logged and slept especially hard. In the middle of the night I was wakened by an eerie wail. It did not come from any of us and went on and on. At first I thought it must be from a passing pod of Blues.

I chose a friend to go with me and, leaving my father in charge, followed the cry through the darkness. When first light came we called out to the passer-by, but got no answer except the same wailing sound. Drawing close we found a single Blue swimming back the way we'd come, toward warmer waters. He didn't slow down as we hove alongside. He was an uncanny sight: his eyes were open and blank. He looked blind, yet obviously could see, for he turned when I swam in front of him.

He ignored our questions, continuing the same eerie lament. Finally my companion Krūga, one of the Council, took me aside. "I have seen the likes of this only once before," he said grimly. "He is crazed. His mind has ceased to work. Something terrible has happened, for he is not himself and will not be for awhile. Let us return to the pod."

When we told the rest of the Council, all were unnerved by the news, and none could explain it. Whales rarely lose their minds. None beside Krūga had seen any creature act without reason, except sharks. We decided to post an extra lookout that day and not to sleep on the surface that night.

The day passed without further incident and we relaxed somewhat. We swam along the krill beds until we sighted green mountains of ice on the horizon. The ice field was protection if we needed it. My heart rejoiced at the sight and I wondered if we would see our friends again this year—especially Ala and Ali. The albatrosses added to our security. I looked forward to the beautiful spirals they described rising high above us to keep watch miles in every direction.

It was with pleasant talk of Ala and Ali that Lewtë and I settled to sleep under the surface that night.

Just before dawn, as I was rising for air, I heard the first propeller. It was still dark, but from the sound I guessed the ship was far off and not headed directly toward us. Yet, it was between us and the ice fields. I quietly sank down to the others, letting them sleep while I listened.

But I was wide awake with concern. Though one ship didn't necessarily mean whalers, I had never before seen a ship in these waters. The sound didn't recede. I listened, perfectly still. Suddenly my heart sank. The sound had changed subtly; the ship had altered direction and was heading toward us. I woke

Lewtë. We nudged everybody awake, making the sign for silence. Together we listened fearfully and soon heard the whine of a second propeller.

Cautiously we rose and heard, as we did, a third and a fourth propeller join the first two. As we surfaced our worst fears were realized. It was a sight to chill the stoutest heart. Near the horizon, under red and green running lights, cruised four whalers between us and the safety of the ice. Worse, behind them, lit up like a small city, loomed the vast silhouette of a factory ship that swallowed whales whole. They were headed directly toward us. As if to underscore this murderous sight, the sun rose, a sullen streak of red.

We couldn't be absolutely sure they'd spotted us, though I guessed that was why they had changed direction. But on the faint chance they hadn't, we dove and swam desperately at a right angle to their course. The propellers faded and we began to hope we had lost them, when, as one, they swung toward us. And now they increased their speed.

Those were a difficult few seconds. I recalled the harpoon tearing my flesh and the whalers pursuing me. I recalled the line of ships strung across the bay and the endless explosions. I knew that man, with his fast ships able to listen underwater, could follow us anywhere; that no whale could swim fast enough or deep enough or hold his breath long enough to escape the whaling fleet; that our only hope was to get under the ice. Now the mystery of the lone Blue whale was solved. No doubt these same whalers had destroyed his pod and, their cruel appetite glutted, let him go, a crazed derelict, to cruise the lonely deeps. At that moment I felt close to panicking, but knew that others were looking to me for hope, for reassurance. I clenched my jaws, pressing my tongue to the roof of my mouth.

In a calm tone I spoke to the Council. We couldn't reach the ice without surfacing to breathe. If we swam directly for it, the whalers would catch us when we came up for air. Quickly we realized our only chance lay in working our way around the fleet by a zigzag course. We agreed to spread out and surface only when absolutely necessary. Each calf would swim by its mother.

At my whistle we were off, swimming silently. Each time we zigged or zagged, the propellers faded for a moment and our hopes rose, only to be dashed as the ships changed course too. We swam as fast as we could, but the ships swam faster. Slowly they gained on us.

For several hours we led them in a chase around a wide half circle. Despite our best maneuvering, they stayed between us and the ice field, closing the distance by half. The calves began to tire. I myself was short of breath. As I surfaced for the third time, I glimpsed the killer ships bearing down on us, only miles away. In the bright daylight I caught from the nose of each the glint of a harpoon gun.

I felt no fear, but despair filled my stomach. Eventually we would be forced to surface near them. Had I gone on the Lonely Cruise, rescued Lewtë, and returned to lead the pod only to see us all destroyed by whalers? I had failed Hralekana's command to guard well cow and calf. It didn't make sense—yet I knew that men were bent on erasing us from the blue earth. All of this flashed through my mind as I watched the ships draw closer, the machinery inside them rattling for the kill.

I felt a nudge. It was Lewtë. She looked terribly sad and drawn but managed a smile. "Remember when we took the Plunge, how it seemed we were leaving behind everything we loved?" she asked. "It seemed like we were going down into a blackness beyond recall, and yet . . ."

She stopped. I knew what she meant. I couldn't say anything for the lump in my throat, yet I smiled back and felt lighter. The Plunge . . . oh, how I wished we could take the Plunge now! But even if the calves could join us, the ships would still be there when we rose. I remembered how the cold and blackness was suddenly transformed into the warm Ocean of Light and recalled the Bright Presence in that Ocean. For a moment I felt strangely free in spirit. "The Whale of Light," I said to myself, "he'd give the whalers something to think about!"

It was then the idea came. It was a reckless idea, a mad one, and probably wouldn't do any good—but that didn't matter, because it was our only chance, even if a foolish one.

I submerged and called the Council to me. When they heard my plan they protested, as I knew they would. Lewtë broke into a shrill cry and turned away. My father pled with me. Calmly, ignoring my father and Lewtë, I explained once again that my unusual size might create enough of a diversion to allow the others to escape. If my plan worked they just might have enough time to swim around the fleet to the ice fields.

Then, as leader, I commanded it be done.

Time was of the essence. For a few seconds I clung to the speechless Lewtë and then, avoiding my parents' eyes, rushed to the surface, leaping as high as I could—twelve fathoms out of the water. I made an enormous splash the whalers couldn't miss if they'd been ten miles distant, not just one. Then I swam to meet them head-on. At first I couldn't tell if the plan was working. I hoped the pod would take air quickly and vanish underwater, swinging wide around the fleet. My heart lifted when I saw the four harpoon ships close ranks. As I hoped, the sight of a large Humpback breaching excited the hunters and each raced to have first shot at me.

The water broke in white wings against each thin bow as it bent toward me. I heard chains rattle and saw figures running about the nose of each ship where the harpoons glinted. Soon I heard the shouts of men.

The waves shone emerald, with frothy caps; the sky,

blue and sun-drenched. Now that I had made the decision and given the pod hope, I felt exhilarated. My despair was entirely gone. Sun glinted from the white-caps. It was a fine morning on which to die. I felt a tremendous defiance of steel ships and cruel men rise up within me. The lust of battle was upon me—the joy of the terrible Leviathan who haunts the dreams of men. I could do little to stop those steel prows—that I knew—but perhaps I could dent one, and the decoy action would save cow and calf. For this I had been made. I felt rise within me the joy of being, and with it a cry from my whole nature—a wave-shattering bellow to rattle the heads of men listening in the ships. Then I began my death song.

The whalers were only a mile off, the four prows racing with less than a ship's length between them. I could see a harpooner standing behind each cannon and I sang to give courage to the others now skirting the fleet:

> For this moment was I made and no other moment—
> To sing my whalesong wild on the wave
> Under blowing sky, green sea, and leaping sun.
> Remember well, cow and calf, as you cruise the years
> The joy of the father as he flashed in the fray.

The sun glittering on wave and harpoon, together with the joy of battle, played tricks with my eyes—or so it seemed. As I drew near the ships, plunging through each wave, I saw something glow far down on

129

the ocean floor. Under each wave the glow was bigger, rising between me and the ships. I blinked even as I sang, wondering what was wrong with my eyes. Then it filled the ocean before me.

The glow broke the waves in front of me, rising up and up. This happened very fast, but at the moment it took forever. An expanse of white loomed, drawing itself higher and higher until it blocked out the ships and blue sky. I drew in my breath and still it came, in one effortless sweep upward. At length sky shone under it an instant, together with the ships, just before I saw arch over me the largest pair of flukes imaginable.

I didn't know what to think—I had no time to think. The sky crashed between the ships and me. The crash was deafening and the white crest from it flipped me over. When I opened my eyes again, there, facing the fleet, his back to me, was Hralekana.

At least it *looked* like Hralekana, but now he was mostly white. I remembered the strange white patches I'd seen in his cave. But then he'd been covered with mossy barnacles. These he'd shaken off, revealing his albino skin. I now recalled the calf's rhyme which my mother sang,

> *Around and over and under the sea,*
> *Come, O come, White Whale to me,*

and knew it was not a rhyme just for calves.

130

"Hralekana!" I called out, but he was already swimming toward the ships and did not heed me. "Hralekana!" sang a chorus of voices behind me. I looked and there were most of the Council and the pod, having surfaced behind me at the great crash. But they received no answer as this Behemoth, churning the water with giant flukes and flippers, sped toward the ships, for a moment blocking them from view.

Over the waves came his reply. First the water around us buzzed, then our skins tingled and our ears hurt from the war cry of that Terror of the Old Whalers, that Wrecker of Wooden Ships, true Leviathan and Kraken of the Deep. It came low, then louder, rising to a mammoth trumpeting that echoed for miles under those seas and buoyed us above the waves. I wondered what the harpooners felt. But steadily the four ships closed on him.

I turned to the pod. "Dive and swim!" I shouted. "Swim for your lives to the ice fields!" The cows and calves submerged immediately. The Council herded the pod along, but I and a few others remained, watching the white form as it closed with the bows of the whalers. Not even imminent death could have driven me from that sight.

A mile away Hralekana swam under the nose of the lead ship; the others trailed it by half a length. He disappeared for a moment and then the sea shook with an enormous, resonant thump. The ship rose a fathom out of the water and settled, its top shaking. Two men fell from the railings into the sea. A few seconds later the shape of Hralekana floated to the surface, stunned, nearly as long as the ship itself. We heard a sharp *boom* and saw a flash of fire and smoke. The harpoon sped into his side, uncoiling after it a black rope. The piercing steel woke Hralekana and he thrashed his giant tail against the side of the ship. Men ran every which way, shouting in confusion.

Another explosion shook the water and we watched a second harpoon strike his other side. Hralekana shuddered. Meanwhile the ship had lowered a small boat to pick up the men overboard. With one thrash of his tail he lifted it in the air and dashed it splintering against the starboard hull. Then, as if the harpoons had done no hurt, he pulled in front of the ships, dragging them together. We heard men yell as the two bows drew perilously close. Hralekana heaved harder. There was a loud crunch and rending of metal; men screamed and ran everywhere. Smoke and flames erupted from the bow of one, and both ships cut loose from Hralekana. The burning one began to settle in the bow; the other lowered boats into the water. Meanwhile two more ships moved in.

Why didn't Hralekana escape while he had the chance? "Hralekana!" we called in vain. The White Whale rolled over and turned toward the attacking ships. We saw two red streaks where blood flowed down his sides.

One explosion followed another as the two new

ships speared him on opposite sides. The Great Whale rose up in the water, thrashing his tail against the side of one, rolling and tangling himself in the rope. The ship backed up and let out more line, as did the other. With a mighty heave Hralekana reversed direction and tried to pull these ships together, as he had the first two. But these ships continued to let out line. We now counted four red streaks running down his watery sides.

The new harpoons had struck vital parts, for Hralekana thrashed in pain as he attempted to draw the ships after him. They did give, by inches, but their propellers spun in reverse, drawing back on the cruel harpoons.

Only then did Hralekana begin his death song. He rose thrashing and leaped partway out of the water, tangling himself further in the ropes. The blood striped him round and round as he rolled, but his song was loud and sharp with an edge of joy. All of us held our breath to listen.

> Now does Hralekana heave into the heavens,
> Who long lay alone, lurking in darkness
> Piercing in thought the plight of his people,
> Listening for the light to illuminate all.
> Long had he warred against whaler and wooden ship
> Only to steer from the fatal strength of steel.
> Now one last time he whelms the wave
> Driven by the word that delved through his dream:
> "By losing all things you will lead into life

133

A pod in peril. They will find new power.
Though the steel harpoon cut home to your heart,
Your ransom will render new life to the remnant.
Then shall you swim in that bright Ocean
Where shows no sorrow nor shadow of turning.''

He lay still for a while, and then we saw the death pangs shudder through him. Without his noticing, the mammoth factory ship had moved up behind him, its white top shining like a ghastly city. One harpoon ship had sunk. The two attached to Hralekana backed off to make room for the factory ship. We heard the rattle of chains as its huge and terrible mouth opened to swallow Hralekana and rend him to pieces.

We could hardly bear to watch, but at that moment he came to life one last time. He fought, and rolled, and thrashed, and tried to plunge. His song was faint now, but just as triumphant, as he sang of the Light. So violent was his thrashing that the water around him foamed red with blood and the factory ship had to back off three times. We could not bear to watch that final act and started slowly after the others—now far under the ice. But Hralekana's voice rose to one last ecstatic note, and we turned to witness him spout his last breath. All of us were struck to the heart, for we saw his spout rise high into the air, higher than the ship, tinged with the blood he was shedding for us, a rose-red fountain over a bloody sea.

Eleven

Enormous green jewels of ice covered us as we plunged deep, deep in our sorrow. None said a word, the last notes of Hralekana's death song still ringing in our ears, the sight of that rose-red fountain impressed on our eyes forever. Under berg after berg we swam to lose the whalers in the field of ice.

In the silence I heard a faint vibration that grew to a humming and then to a medley of various strains—the singing of the ice. But my mind was black with grief and at first I didn't listen. Hralekana had died in agony and not one of us had moved a fluke to help him. I wanted to sink into darkness and never rise again to view blue sky or green wave, since they had let themselves be covered with the blood of one so fearless and fine. All had betrayed him; the whales, the sky, the great ocean itself had betrayed him. We had let Hralekana die.

Bitter tears flowed.

Meanwhile the singing of the ice grew insistent. I ignored it, wanting to be alone with my grief. It grew louder, however, as if it held some message for me. I listened for a moment. Slowly a memory broke through my grief: I was back in the cave again as Hralekana's voice resounded: "Guard well cow and calf, and in danger *seek the singing of the ice at the end of the world.*" At last it dawned on me: the prophecy uttered by Hralekana years back had come true. And I knew then that he had foreseen all this, including his death. The blackness passed from my mind. I felt comforted, though an even bigger lump swelled in my throat and my tears flowed in two oily streams.

My weeping was interrupted by a sudden squall of happy whistles and trills. We had come upon the others, safely at rest in water surrounded on all sides by ice. Great then was our mingled joy and our sorrow. Lewtë and I nuzzled for a long time, the sea slick with our tears. My father and mother wept with relief.

Later I heard three sharp squawks and looked up through my tears to see three graceful forms circling us. In my grief I had forgotten to look for Ala, but there he was with Ali and another beautiful bird. It was the awkward Ross, full grown.

I spouted the joy and sadness of our reunion while the three tenderly pecked barnacles and told me how they'd searched for us to warn us of the whalers.

"When I saw the ships cluster, I was afraid they'd found you before we had," Ala said. "If it hadn't been for the white whale, we would have arrived too late."

I told them about Hralekana. They stood by my blowhole, transfixed. Even Ross hardly twitched a feather. Afterwards Ala remarked grimly that more than one ancestor of his had been cruelly shot by man.

"And not for food," he added, "but for wicked sport—in one case after guiding the man's ship through the ice." He fell silent at the memory of this ancient injury to his clan.

At last Ala spread his wings. "We will stay with you," he promised, "and be your eyes so that the whalers will not surprise you again."

That whole day and the next the pod mourned Hralekana, singing a lament. In it we chronicled what we knew of his life, and our sorrow was eased and turned to joy. We saw how Hralekana had freely chosen his death—had even foreseen it—and, indeed, as one of the Great Ones, the White Whales who live for hundreds of years, was created for just such an end.

For days we lurked by the ice, swimming between the green mountains as they sang, whined, and growled, grinding together in that sweet cold water. Ala and his family were as good as their word and led us out to beds of krill when it was safe, circling above us all the while.

The whaling fleet remained in the neighborhood a few days, undoubtedly expecting as to reappear. But at last they steamed back to warmer waters. The albatrosses followed them a good distance, returning to say the ocean was now clear for hundreds of miles. So we slept again in the krill beds.

Lewtë had grown ungainly heavy and ate even at night, waking me with a nudge to go with her into the krill. She was quieter now and spent much time alone, a lovely smile on her face, dreaming of the calf that was to be.

One noon something gleamed on the horizon. Flashing over the water a pair of dolphins approached —our old friends Marmo and Scallop. Once they'd caught their breath, it took them forever to stop interrupting each other. What they told us we already knew—the story of our encounter with the whalers, of my decision to face them alone, and of Hralekana's going in my place. For once, nothing was exaggerated in the telling, though I corrected them on one or two fine points.

They stayed several days, giving us news of the Seven Seas. The whaling fleet, they said, was back in port early this year. And there were fewer fleets out. The number had been dwindling for several years. There was some hope in that, though man was always unpredictable.

One night, a week after Hralekana's death, he appeared to me in a vision. It might have been a dream, except that it was sharper and clearer than a dream, and I recall waking beforehand.

In it Hralekana appeared glowing from the bottom of the sea. This time he was not reflecting sunlight, but radiated light from within. I would have thought he was the Whale of Light, except he had Hralekana's features. It is not lawful to repeat all that he told me, but he gave me great hope. His mouth broke into a radiant smile, showing yards of dazzling baleen, as he told me that one day man would no longer hunt whales, and—what's more—would live at peace with all creatures. He said the Whale of Light himself had promised this and that he had done—or was doing—something among men to bring it to pass. He even indicated that man was absolutely crucial to the future of the earth and that everything depended upon him.

Next Hralekana smiled even more broadly, if that were possible, and looked kindly on me, and on Lewtë where she slept next to me. The Whale of Light, he said, had informed him that a great honor was soon to be ours.

He faded and I found myself very much awake. I woke Lewtë and told her of the vision. She smiled, snuggled up to me, and went back to sleep.

Great was our play and joy in those cold seas after the whalers left. Lewtë and I would leap in the air together (not very high because of her condition) while the three albatrosses circled around us shrieking with laughter. One day months later a feeling of urgency came upon the pregnant cows. It was time to swim to warmer waters and the safe nesting shallows. By now Lewtë was so round I wondered that she could move at all. Following a great feast of krill, we took off slowly for the warm seas and perfumed air of the tropics.

After weeks of clear weather and an easy voyage we were at last in the safe shallows of our birth. Within two weeks all the other cows gave birth, but Lewtë continued to grow bigger and bigger. I became concerned and hardly slept, carrying food to Lewtë, who now stayed in one place. I was aided by Lunau, a childless female who wanted to assist at the birth and to help watch over the newborn. I was becoming quite anxious. My parents and Lunau tried to calm me.

One night Lunau wakened me, excited. I looked over at Lewtë where she lay at the surface, breathing hard and looking very weak.

Scared, I swam over to her and gently stroked her side. For several hours she labored, unable to speak, while I stroked and sang. The birth was difficult. Then her body moved in mighty contractions. I held her as best I could with my flippers. After what seemed forever, from beneath her stomach protruded a small pair of flukes. Lunau lay close to her and sang to the flukes, every once in a while nudging Lewtë's belly. Slowly, inch by inch, tail-first, came the body of a large male calf. As soon as he was free, Lunau pushed him to the surface so he could begin to breathe. She held him up as his eyes opened and his flukes and flippers began to move.

I lay speechless while Lewtë smiled proudly at me. She was too weak to swim, though otherwise unhurt. But the calf! Not only was he larger than any newborn we'd ever seen, but from the tip of his nose to the end of his flukes he was foam-white.

At that moment he uttered his first high-pitched whistle, slapping the water with his little tail. Lewtë and I smiled. Suddenly, without saying it, each of us knew what his name would be.

"Hralekana," we whispered together. I swam over to him.

"Hralekana," I breathed into his tiny ear.

I nuzzled our calf and nuzzled Lewtë until both fell asleep and Lunau shooed me away. Then in my joy I swam off alone under the stars to sing my song. At dawn I began the song of my life and sang it all day and well into this night.

This is my song, as it is up to now—and, thanks to the Whale of Light, not yet ended.

So rests the song of Hrūnakyana—the song of a whale.

May the Humpbacks sing their song forever!